POLE POSITION

KRISTIAN PARKER

Queens Crescent

Christmas at Queens Crescent

Pole Position

With Pride Publishing

Village Affairs

The Rule of Three

Three's Company

Triple Intent

Speak Its Name

To Light a Fire

Call it Love

Spotlight on Love

Collections

My Bloody Valentine: Venetian Valentine

Summer Collection: Sun, Sea and Spotted Squid

Pole Position

First edition

Published 2023 by Kristian Parker

Copyright © 2023 Kristian Parker

To Heidi, my ride or die. We have been through so much together and I'm a lucky man indeed to have you. Love you forever, sidekick.

CHAPTER ONE

"Formula One is a cutthroat business. I'm old news."

"And how does that make you feel, Charles?"

How did she think it made him feel? "Like shit. That's why I've signed with South Tel."

Sylvia sat back in her chair and took off her glasses. "When did you decide this?"

Charles' hackles started to rise. "About a month ago."

She looked surprised. "We've had three sessions in that time. Didn't you want to talk about it?"

Charles Worthington had been coming to this tastefully decorated office for almost twelve months. He knew every framed watercolour and tasteful yet bland fabric off by heart.

In the time he had been coming here, he'd laid himself totally bare. Charles had felt out of control more often than he had expected. It reminded him of all those times he'd been sent to the headmaster's office. Now he knew he had to become the captain of his own ship again.

He'd had enough of talking.

"To be honest, not really. I know I'm going to be tested. Believe me, I've thought about it," he blurted out. "But if I don't go back now, I'm done. I've missed one season and I'm thirty-five years old. Those are not great negotiating chips. If I add another season to it, I won't get a place in a go kart competition."

Sylvia rubbed the bridge of her nose. "I get it, Charles," she said. "I do. There's a lot of money involved, but..."

He sat forward. "You think this is about the cash? I've more money than I know what to do with. I need to go out on a high. Can't you see? Not pissed up in the gutter outside Libertine."

She smiled sadly at him. "Fine, I can see you're going to do this, and our time is ending. All I can say to you is please keep up our appointments and your AA meetings. Time will get precious for you, but you must be wise."

Charles nodded. "I know that. Believe me, I do. I'm not going back there. I can do it."

Sylvia didn't reply. She simply stood, to indicate it was time for him to leave. As he got to the door, he turned. "I won't be able to do it without you," he said. "I need to know you're with me."

"You can rely on yourself now," Sylvia replied. "But for the record, I'm with you."

It was all he needed to hear.

As he jogged down the steps of the Harley Street practice, Will was leaning against Charles' Maserati. His pride and joy.

"Get a shift on, big bro," Will said. "We're late."

Charles glanced at his watch. Shit, they were. "Get in," he said.

Once in the driver's seat, he fired up the ridiculously expensive car and veered out into the London traffic. "How long have we got?"

"About thirty minutes," Will said, fiddling with the in-car system. "Forty if you don't mind a frosty reception."

Will finished typing the details into the sat nav. It told them it would take forty-five minutes.

"Bastard," Will shouted.

Charles started to weave expertly in between traffic. He got a few horns blared at him for his trouble.

"Wind your window down," Will said. "They'll shit themselves when they see it's the great Charles Worthington."

"Being Charles Worthington works against me these days."

They drove in silence for a few minutes. Charles lost himself in controlling the car. It had always been his happy place.

"How are you going to play it?" Will said. "With South Tel, I mean."

Charles had no idea how to answer this question. He'd been out of the game for a bit. Watching a Netflix documentary and gossiping with friends was not the same as feeling the vibe, race after race. "I don't know," he said, sharply. "Give me some peace to think about it."

As they dashed into the cavernous chrome offices of South Tel Formula One, a party of three waited for them at reception. None of them looked very happy.

"Jesus Christ," Charles said, under his breath. "We did it in thirty-five. They look like I'm a day late."

He straightened his collar and slowed his walk down.

"Meera," he said.

"You're late."

Meera Jakhar, the CEO with a formidable reputation. A stunning woman in her mid-forties, she had risen like a rocket.

"I'm so sorry." Charles panted. "London traffic."

He flashed his dazzling smile. Meera appraised him for a second before turning to a stern man to her left. A man Charles knew only too well.

"Barnaby," Charles said, sticking out his hand. "So good to see you again."

Barnaby Weber was the Team Principal of South Tel Formula One. He could make or break Charles' career. Whilst he had brokered the finer points of their deal, he had made it clear in the press that he didn't fully support the move. It made things awkward to say the least.

It had also made Charles regret losing his manager. Another entry on a long list of stupid things he had to make up for.

"Charles," Barnaby said, with a poker face.

"And I'm Miriam." A flustered young woman with platinum-blonde hair and a clipboard said. They all looked at her. "I'm Mrs Jakhar's assistant."

She had gone a funny shade of beetroot.

"Very pleased to meet you," Charles said.

This only served to make her blush all the more.

"Shall we go?" Meera said.

Miriam dashed over to press the elevator call button.

"You need to make some changes down here," Will said.

Meera stared as if noticing him for the first time. "I'm sorry?"

Will pointed to two huge photographs dominating the reception area. One of the outgoing, Clarence Dupont, and the other of Charles' new teammate, Luis Salvatore.

All part of the elite group of racing car drivers, their paths had crossed many times. Formula One was a small world. He didn't care about Dupont. A life in Formula Two beckoned for him after a disastrous season.

As for Salvatore, Charles couldn't take his eyes from the image. He might have spectacular boyish good looks, but everyone knew Luis to be the dullest person in motorsport. He had never attended a function or been spotted in a trendy bar.

"Dupont," Will said, bringing Charles firmly back to earth. "I would have thought you'd have taken him down by now."

Charles wanted to slap him. "I'm sorry, Mrs Jakhar," he said. "My brother hasn't been house trained yet."

"It's Meera," she answered him. "We have a photo shoot arranged for you and Luis tomorrow. I trust that will be in order."

Mercifully the elevator arrived, and Charles allowed himself to be ushered inside. "There's really no rush," he said as genially as possible. "I'm just happy to be here."

The glass elevator swept them up through a central column to the offices proper.

"Wow, Meera," Will said. "You have quite an operation here."

"I think perhaps you will stick with Mrs Jakhar," she said, before glancing at Charles. He detected the trace of a glint in her eye. "There has to be a line."

Charles could barely contain his amusement as Will looked fit to burst.

Before the air got thicker than a mud bath, the elevator pinged, signalling they had made it to the top floor.

"Come," Meera commanded.

Once more he followed in her slipstream as she swept along the corridor. He noted how everyone stood up a little straighter. Even though she absolutely terrified him, he found himself drawn to her.

The boardroom was packed. Meera made a point of introducing him to everyone, and all the while, Barnaby hovered on the edge. He was making Charles nervous.

Luckily, he'd met some of the people during the negotiations, so he made a beeline for them. There were also a good few people new to him. He'd have to spend time forging relationships. That came naturally to Charles—he never had a problem finding something in common with people.

Will had taken a seat at the back next to Miriam. He nodded and gave Charles a thumbs-up. Charles nodded back.

His brother could be an insufferable twat at times but it grounded Charles to have him there.

"I didn't think you would be up to this."

Charles turned to find Barnaby next to him again. "I think you've made that clear." Charles smiled. "I will prove you wrong."

"That's what Meera said," Barnaby replied.

If the ultimate boss believed in him, that made Charles feel slightly more secure.

"Anyway," Barnaby continued. "Come with me."

He led him towards a cluster of people over by the window. The crowd parted and there was Luis Salvatore...although he didn't look like the scrawny kid who had started becoming a real threat in Charles' last season. He had buffed up and had a brand-new haircut which framed his tan face. His body filled a white T-shirt and jeans perfectly. Even his skin glowed in a way Charles had never noticed before.

In other words, Luis Salvatore had started to earn serious money.

"Luis," Charles said, shaking his hand. "Good to see you again. I'm very excited to be working together."

Luis gave him a kilowatt beam of a smile. Charles made a mental note to book in for more teeth whitening treatment. It seemed to be a big thing at South Tel.

"Charles," Luis replied. "I'm sure you will settle in very well."

He was stunning. Charles hadn't missed out in the looks department. But Luis' beauty seemed to radiate from within. Even so, he had a wariness in his eyes which confused Charles.

"I hope we're ready for some wins," Charles said, glancing at Barnaby.

"Absolutely." Luis grinned.

Charles was at a loss of what to say next. Thankfully, Meera gave him a way out as she took her place at the head of the table. Everyone found seats and when she sat, they all did.

"Right, let's get going," she said, steepling her fingers. "Firstly, I would like to formally welcome Charles Worthington to our little family."

A ripple of comment swept around the room. To Charles' relief, most people seemed friendly except for a young man next to Luis. Charles clocked his sour glare immediately.

As all eyes were on Charles, he realised a few words were in order. "Thank you, Meera," he said. "Most of you will know I'm no stranger to being the new kid on the block."

A few people chuckled. Charles had driven for all the teams in the top five. He had become known as "One Contract Worthington" in the media for his penchant for change.

"And I have no doubt you will know why I missed last season. The press covered it enough."

Shots of him being driven to rehab haunted him to this day.

"I'm not going to stand in front of you and pretend I haven't had my problems. I am fully appreciative of the gamble you are all taking on me. I look forward to repaying your kindness on the track."

A couple of people clapped, which made him feel more foolish than complete silence would have.

"I don't have to tell you that a fourth finish last season is not good enough," Meera said. "Dupont's disastrous performance meant that the work fell to Luis." She appraised the young driver like a lioness viewing her favourite cub. "With two top class drivers, number one is the only goal this year," she continued. "Now let's get down to business."

The day stretched on. By the time Charles and Will got to Charles' house, he was absolutely done in.

"Fucking hell," Charles said. "I reckon we've met every bugger in the building today."

He flopped down on the sofa and accepted the fizzy water Will handed to him. His lounge had recently been redecorated in golds and whites—the decorator vowed it would be a lot more calming than the lurid party room he'd had for ten years.

"Don't worry, I got all the names down," Will said, cracking open a beer. "I'll test you on the flight."

Charles had a superpower of forgetting people's names, often within seconds. Will came in handy at times.

"Who was that number sucking lemons next to Salvatore?" Charles asked, kicking off his shoes.

He hadn't been able to ignore the glare coming from that part of the table. When he made an enemy, he preferred to know why.

"Paulo Ribeiro," Will said, glancing at his phone. "Luis' assistant and childhood friend."

"Oh, God." Charles said, covering his face with his hands. He's got a Will."

Will threw a cushion at him. "He's his friend, not his brother, thank you."

Charles went to stand by the window. His first-floor drawing room overlooked Queens Crescent—dubbed Billionaire's Row in the press—a half-moon street of Georgian townhouses that curved around gardens. He had absolutely fallen in love with the place as soon as he'd walked onto the private road.

Each house was painted a brilliant white with shiny gloss black railings. Woe betide any resident who didn't have that refreshed at least once a year. It could be a competitive street. Charles had learnt that the first summer he'd lived here when he hadn't bothered to put any window boxes out. Now he paid someone a lot of money to make sure the exterior of his house was fit for inspection.

Charles had lived there over ten years. It afforded him a decent level of privacy while still being in the centre of his home city. Of course, he had a couple of other places. One in the Wiltshire countryside and a small penthouse in Nice. However, Queens Crescent felt like home, and he'd made some decent friends amongst the neighbours. Something that never happened in the big city. Most people lived next door to someone for years and still couldn't recognise them in the supermarket.

"I want you to give Meera a wide berth," Charles said.

"Calm down," Will exclaimed. "I'll have her eating out of my hand in no time."

Charles spun around. "I mean it, Will. She's fucking amazing and can see right through you. Leave her to me."

Will flung his phone down on the sofa. When Charles had taken him on as his assistant, it had been the perfect way to have someone to rely on. Charles suspected he had his eye on filling the manager vacancy. Never in a million years would Charles let that happen. Will didn't always think through the consequences of his actions and had landed them in hot water on more than one occasion.

"You fucked things up at Dream Tech by shagging Veronica," Charles replied.

Will sighed. They had had this conversation many times and it still wound Charles up. Will being caught in bed with the boss's daughter. It had sent shockwaves through the team and nearly got Will beaten up.

"Don't start that shit again. I couldn't be expected to know old Dimitri would take it so bad?"

Flopping down on the sofa again, Charles sighed. "Greek fathers are protective of their daughters, you prick. Anyway, I'm not getting into that, so just do as I say. Stick to sorting out what we need and leave the management to me."

Will scowled. "What did you make of Mr Team Principal

himself?" he asked. "He might have given you a warmer welcome."

"Listen," Charles said. "We all know what I was like before...last season. He's probably worried I'll be pissed up by the time we make it to Monaco."

Charles understood Barnaby had to focus on delivering a cohesive team. Salvatore had been with South Tel long enough that they knew how he ticked. An ex-boozer like Charles, who had spent more time on the front pages for his sex life than his podium wins, must be giving him sleepless nights.

"I liked Salvatore though," Charles continued. "Did you?"

"I think he'll be a problem if you want the truth."

Dupont had been the number one driver at South Tel and Luis had been with them for his whole driving career. Barnaby wouldn't be good at his job if he didn't have nerves about a new dynamic. Considering Dupont's woeful finish at the end of last season, they should be kissing his feet.

"Another one to leave to me then," Charles mused.

"The gay driver," Will replied. "I'm sure you can get him on side."

Charles threw the pillow back at Will. "I'll use my charm, not my cock."

"Right, I'm heading out," Will said, getting to his feet. "Coming?"

Charles shook his head. They had the photo shoot tomorrow and he intended on getting eight hours sleep for that.

"Take her to your place as well," he shouted after Will. "I'm not running a fucking boarding house. Who is it anyway?"

"Miriam."

"Oh, for fuck's sake, Will."

"Relax," he said with a grin. "It's just a drink. You know I'd never compromise a lady."

Charles gave him a middle finger salute and shuddered as

he heard him thundering down the oak staircase. He would come through that one day.

His mind drifted to Luis Salvatore. The beautiful man who the press worshipped for his bravery at never hiding his sexuality. He had been an enigma to Charles for a few years.

He couldn't be that boring in real life. It would be crime to be that gorgeous and as dull as the stories said. Time would tell.

CHAPTER TWO

In the photographer's changing room, Charles zipped up the mint and white jumpsuit. It clung to him in all the right places. They had measured him the day he had signed his contract, and whoever made their suits were geniuses.

Checking himself out in the mirror, Charles thought he scrubbed up all right. At thirty-five, his thick blond curls showed no sign of grey. The wrinkles at the side of his eyes had been eradicated with a quick dose of Botox. His skin looked healthy and bronzed for the first time in years.

As he walked out of the cubicle, he bumped into Luis, who looked just as handsome as the day before with his tan skin and dark hair cut short. It was his gleaming smile that made Charles go weak at the knees though. "Oh, hello again," Charles said thrusting his hand out.

"Charles." Luis took Charles' hand and shook it. He had a strong grip along with his deep blue eyes that currently had Charles transfixed.

"Ready to say cheese?" Charles asked.

"Cheese?" Luis frowned. "Oh, you mean the photos. In Brazil we say *sorriso*. To smile. But yes, it's a necessary evil."

They walked down the corridor into the photographer's loft

studio. Daniel French had achieved legendary status in fashion circles. Charles had been astounded when Meera had announced she had commissioned him to do the promo shots. It suggested a different approach from other teams. He quite liked this—it seemed fitting as Charles had a completely different mindset from when he'd raced with other teams.

"Charlie boy," Daniel shouted.

Instantly, Charles recoiled. He and Daniel had moved in similar circles over the years. Daniel always had a different model on his arm, and he'd seen Charles as something of a kindred spirit. "Hello, Daniel," he replied.

He glanced nervously at Luis, who regarded him with interest. Luis did not have a reputation of enjoying the high life. He would race, then disappear to his hotel room. Charles couldn't remember ever seeing him at a dinner function.

"All right," Daniel said, clapping his hands together. "Let's take Luis first, then Charles. We'll do the crappy promo shit first then I thought we'd go a bit off piste with some buddy shots. How does that sound?"

Luis smirked at Charles. "You reckon we can be buddies?"

"It's just a matter of time," Charles replied with a wink.

He sat down on a brocade sofa that someone had kindly placed against a wall, facing the action. As he watched Luis walk onto the set, he took in his frame. The suit clung to him like a second skin. There was more than a hint of a muscular body under there.

The curves of his arse made Charles lick his lips. He imagined what it would be like unzipping him and revealing all that gorgeous honey-coloured skin. The thought made his cock twitch and he remembered that his own suit didn't leave much to the imagination. He did not want to go and get his photo taken with an erection.

Making a concerted effort to think pure thoughts, he watched Luis striking a series of ill-at-ease poses. He would show him what to do when he had his turn. For now, he remained content to watch from the side-lines.

And watch he did as Daniel had Luis making all sorts of different shapes.

"That's it, Luis," Daniel coaxed. "Raise your hands as though you've just won Monaco."

"Again," Luis said, drily.

Luis stretched his arms up. Charles couldn't take his eyes off his body.

Eventually, he and Luis swapped places. It might have been in Charles' imagination, but he could have sworn Luis brushed past him when he had absolutely no need to. The scent of Luis' spicy cologne filled his nostrils. Without thinking, Charles breathed it in. He caught Luis watching him with amusement. Blushing, he took his place in front of the camera.

"Okay, Charles," Daniel bellowed. He wasn't a quiet man. "Remember that time we took those models to Biarritz?"

Charles shuddered. It had been a free trip organised by a sports magazine. They had got some decent shots, but unfortunately, the endless flow of champagne also resulted in Charles throwing up in Daniel's camera bag and being thrown out of a club for picking a fight with some snap-happy tourists.

"Don't remind me," Charles replied. "Those days are long gone."

Daniel looked aghast. "The alcohol industry mourns your passing."

Charles made a face and got himself ready. He glanced over at Luis, who was regarding him with a serious expression. "Everything okay?" he asked.

"Of course," Luis replied. "Just watching the master at work."

The words were dripping with sarcasm. Charles' reputation clearly preceded him. Perhaps it wouldn't just be Barnaby who posed a problem.

The next few days passed in a whirlwind of press interviews, more photo shoots and a meeting with his public relations advisor about a potential new collaboration with an electronics manufacturer.

The first race of the season was less than two weeks away and they were due to fly out to Bahrain in three days for preseason testing. They'd already had a weekend of it in the South of France and Charles had handled the new car like a dream.

When Charles had first got into the cockpit, he'd panicked that the skills had left him. Once out on the track, the relief that this wasn't the case had almost made him cry.

As he glided up and down his basement swimming pool, Charles tried to put all the concerns and noise out of his mind. In the built-up centre of London, homeowners were desperate for space. Instead of adding floors, a lot of people dug down to extend the size of their homes.

Charles had been an early adopter of this craze. He had created a bubble from the world with a decent-sized pool, jacuzzi, and heated recliners. Charles didn't even allow Will to enter his sanctuary. Once he'd done his twenty lengths, he hopped out. In the distance, his phone was ringing. Let it ring. He needed this relaxation time. The next few months might prove to be the most important of his life.

Just as he lay down to dry off, it started to ring again. "Fuck's sake," he muttered as he threw on a robe. He padded up the stairs to the kitchen, to find his phone vibrating around the table. "Calm the fuck down," he growled, grabbing it.

Luis Salvatore

To his amazement, a jolt of nerves jangled around his body when he saw the name on the caller ID.

"Luis," he said. "And what can I do for you?"

"I know we're off today, but I thought I'd ask you out to lunch."

Charles frowned. Now that was a turn up for the books. "That sounds wonderful," he replied. "Where are you taking me?"

"Wait and see. Be ready for one."

The line went dead.

That kind of shit usually annoyed Charles. Today it served to fire his curiosity. The only pain of it being the fact he had no idea what to wear.

He had less than two hours to get ready.

"Bang goes my relaxing day downstairs," he said.

Ninety minutes later and he was dashing around like a madman, mainly due to the fact he'd spent eighty-five of those minutes trying to settle on the perfect outfit. Determined not to appear as if he'd made too much effort, he went for black jeans and an ice-blue shirt with a darker blue blazer. Set against his tan skin and strawberry blond curls, he looked good in it.

Once he'd tamed a rogue curl on the side of his head that kept insisting on sticking straight up, he grabbed his things and waited. It had been a good while since Charles Worthington had waited for someone. He found he quite liked the idea of being an equal rather than the one everyone relied on for whatever reason. Fame or money, usually both.

His phone buzzed again.

Outside.

He had come early. Had he done that to throw Charles off balance or was he one of those organised and together people? A shudder ran through Charles, who lived his life like the White Rabbit, constantly late for something.

He bounded down the steps where Luis waited in a midnight blue Aston Martin Roadster. Luis popped the passenger door open and Charles sank into the leather seats. "Nice wheels."

"Amazing what you get free when you don't need it," Luis replied.

"What are we doing then?"

Luis gave him a smile and roared the car into life. They set off out of the Crescent. The resident busybody, Mrs Wimpole, would be having something to say about the noise. They weaved through the London traffic. The sunny March day brought much needed light after a dark, miserable winter. Luis had put the top down and more than one person noticed the two famous drivers in a car.

"We'll have the paps on us," Charles warned.

"That's no bad thing," Luis replied. "There's a lot of noise about you coming to South Tel."

Charles stole a glance at him. The Brazilian man had model looks. The papers often described him as having a chiselled jaw and effortless style, and Charles could see why.

He had on a leather jacket and dark jeans, and a diamond ear stud set off his piercing blue eyes. No wonder a legion of fans loved him. He had brought Formula One to a whole new generation.

They parked at a private place near to St Thomas' Hospital, just south of the river.

"The hospital?" Charles asked. "Should I be worried?"

Luis laughed.

Luis led him down to the riverside. The Houses of Parliament stood proudly, dominating the skyline. Even though Charles had lived in the city all his life, the view never failed to impress.

Luis turned right and led him towards Waterloo Bridge.

"You're enjoying this mystery tour, aren't you?" Charles asked.

"I like to keep things exciting," Luis replied.

"I'm sure you do," Charles chuckled. "Providing you're not planning on dumping my body in the river, I can get on board."

They wandered down the pavement. A lot of people were taking in the early spring sunshine, but luckily not many recognised them. Those that did simply waved or stared agog. It wasn't every day people saw two famous drivers sauntering along the Thames.

"I'd never get away with murdering you in broad daylight," Luis said with a smirk. "I'd be careful after dark though."

Charles hadn't expected him to be funny. Whenever he'd seen interviews with Luis, he had been very earnest and keen to make a difference. This side of him remained totally undiscovered by the media. If he were honest, Charles had always written Luis off as dull. He realised he had been very wrong.

They approached the London Eye, the huge Ferris wheel that had been installed on the South Bank to celebrate the turn of the century.

"You first," Luis said, pointing to a booth.

"Are you kidding?"

"No, I reserved us a private pod," Luis replied.

Sure enough, an eager man in his fifties beckoned Charles and Luis over. "Mr Salvatore. Mr Worthington. This is a great honour. I'm a huge fan."

Charles gave his usual vague smile and nodded. Luis, however, went over and shook the man's hand.

"Thank you," he said. "I've never done this before. I'm very much looking forward to it."

The man beamed and stared at Charles expectantly. Charles shook his hand as well. Better late than never, he supposed. "I'm also very excited," he said.

They allowed themselves to be fussed onto the pod.

"We have put some refreshments in a cool box here," the attendant gushed. "And if you need anything at all, there is an intercom by the door. I'll be here." He shut the door behind them, instantly quelling the noises from central London.

"Alone at last, eh?" Charles said. If he focused on the

ground, he could see they were moving. It was almost too slow to notice.

"You want anything?" Luis asked as he opened the cool box. Bottles of champagne, beer and fizzy water lay inside.

"I'll take a water," Charles replied.

Luis frowned. "You don't want anything more exciting? I'm driving, remember."

Shifting uncomfortably, Charles stared out at London that had started to reveal itself as the pod climbed up. "Water's good."

"Oh fuck," Luis replied. "I'm sorry."

"No need," Charles said, truthfully. "Don't get me wrong— every day is a struggle. I can handle it though. I truly believe that." He took the bottle of water Luis offered him. They stood in silence as the pod slowly rose. It wasn't an awkward silence, more companionable.

"I think it's very brave," Luis said, eventually.

"What is?"

"How you've changed your life. It's humbling."

Charles hated compliments about anything other than his driving. He always had. "I just survived. I should never have let it take a hold of me in the first place," he said, swigging the water. "You're the brave one."

As the first openly gay Formula One driver, Luis had received his fair share of ups and downs from the world's press.

"Perhaps we are two heroes?" Luis conceded.

Charles tapped the bottom of his bottle against Luis'. "I'll drink to that."

They watched their ascent in silence for a while. Charles had been on the London Eye when he'd first become famous. Some promotion campaign for a betting company had insisted he and another driver share a cabin with a gaggle of scantily dressed girls. They had drained the bar and taken the girls to a hotel. In those days he believed in giving the people what they wanted.

"Out with it then," Charles said. "You obviously kidnapped me to say something."

Luis sat down on the oval bench in the centre of the pod. He gestured for Charles to sit next to him. "I wanted to speak to you without anyone else overhearing," he began.

"It's all very cloak and dagger," Charles said.

"I know and I'm sorry," Luis replied. "Whilst I admire you, your reputation stands."

In the circles Charles moved in, they didn't do a lot of straight talking like this. Most people kissed his arse. Other drivers had usually been either afraid of him or in awe. Luis appeared to be neither.

He exhaled. "I nearly lost everything when it all came to a head," he explained. "Missing a season while I got myself together nearly finished me off."

"You missed some decent races," Luis replied.

"Yes, and you won a lot of the fuckers."

"Something you made very clear wouldn't have happened if you'd been driving."

It all became clear. A stupidly candid interview he'd done in the media when he'd got out of rehab had made a few waves.

"If you're worried about rivalry, don't be," Charles said. "I'm not here to take you down. I'm here to build me up. I want podium wins again this season. I haven't had one in years."

Luis nodded. "I took us to fourth last year. On my own."

Charles clapped him on the shoulder as he got up. "Then think what we can do, the two of us."

Luis joined him at the glass. "I hope your sentiment is real," he said eventually. "This season is important to me. I don't want to fuck my career up because you need a steppingstone."

Luis' brand of brutal honesty began to grate a little on

Charles. "I'm your teammate, Luis. I'm not your coach. You find and take your own opportunities and I'll take mine."

They were stood close to each other, and Charles smelt the expensive cologne on Luis. A heady mix of spice and woody tones, Charles wondered where the hell he got it from. It certainly wasn't the cheap muck he advertised in airport lounges. Then again, Charles rarely wore the chain store clothes he modelled four times a year.

"I'm not expecting any favours," Luis said. "I simply thought it would be good to chat. The two of us. Paulo thinks I'm mad. He said that you would think I were begging for help."

This Paulo had started to seriously piss Charles off and he'd only met him once. "You shouldn't believe everything you hear," he replied. "A reputation is just that. Look at you, the saint of the poor and the needy. I'm sure even you have an evil side."

Luis grinned. "Oh, I definitely do. I am choosy who I show it to."

It seemed they both had images. The difference being Luis had built a decent one whilst Charles had the fight of his life to escape a shitty one.

It dawned on him that if he and Luis worked together, they might achieve both these aims by the end of the season. "There'll be no drama from me," he said, winking at Luis. "Of that, you have my promise."

Those were famous last words, and he wasn't sure if he even believed them.

But at that moment, as they climbed above London, he desperately wanted them to be true.

CHAPTER THREE

His car sped past the chequered flag like a soaring bird. "Fucking yes!" Charles screamed into his headset. The adrenaline rush of taking it over the line made him want to burst out of his own body.

"Congratulations, Charles," the controller said. "That's a win."

Of course he had bloody won. Jackson Trench, his old enemy, had to settle for second place. By the end of the race, Charles couldn't even see him in his rear-view mirror. Charles had made the perfect start with South Tel. Trench had become a problem during the season Charles had missed. To finally be a contender against him and win was the sweetest taste.

They'd had a vicious war of words in the press. Jackson had accused Charles of bringing the sport into disrepute. He had done it on the day before Charles had gone to rehab. That had smarted. He hoped Jackson was eating his heart out today.

After lapping the course and waving at the cheering crowds, he pulled into the pitstop. Leaping out of the car, he thought the high would never stop. In the old days he would have hit the bar that night to get rid of it. The ever-present temptation still told him to do it. He pushed his feelings down the way he had learnt.

Will dashed over and hugged him. "Nice one," he said, wiping at the tears in his eyes.

Charles lost count of the pats on his back and handshakes as he made his way into his own private area. It was only cordoned off with drapes so even once he got in there, the buzz from the team still came through. Knowing he'd created that made his heart soar. He had missed this feeling so much.

"I bet Trench is spewing," Will crowed. "You want to watch it?"

Charles shook his head. "I'll see him on the podium. That'll be sweet enough."

"There's a dinner tonight. Just the team," Will continued. "You up for it?"

He had planned on a long soak in the bath and a movie. Now that getting steaming drunk was not an option, he supposed he could talk the adrenaline out. God, he felt good right at that moment.

"Yeah, why not?" he replied. "Give me five. Then show me the press."

Will ruffled his hair. "I'll let them know."

Scrubbing his face with his hands, Charles bent over. He hadn't won a race in quite some time, and he'd forgotten the rush. It would have been perfect if Meera had been there to witness it. This would show her she had been right to take a chance on him.

Barnaby and one of his assistants came into the room. "Well done, Charles," he said. "It seems Meera's instincts were right. You were fucking brilliant out there."

Charles hadn't realised how much this had meant to him until doing it. To be returning under the cloud of addiction and South Tel giving him the chance he deserved, he had needed to make an impact. Thank fuck he hadn't had this full epiphany twelve hours before. *A gibbering wreck doesn't win a Grand Prix.*

"Thank you, Barnaby," he replied, unable to stop the huge beam that crept over his face. "It feels good. Thank you for your support even when you weren't sure."

Barnaby narrowed his eyes. "I'm still not one hundred percent sure. Let's say I'm open to persuasion now."

Barnaby had a reputation of being cold as ice. In his world, that was high praise indeed. As Barnaby set off out of the room, Luis stood, waiting in the corridor. Once again, Charles found himself standing taller and puffing his chest out. Why did he care what this guy thought? He had come in first, hadn't he?

"All right, mate?" Charles asked, beaming.

Luis didn't return the smile. "I just want to say congratulations," he said.

"That's very much appreciated," Charles replied, and he meant it. "Fourth for you too. We smashed it today, kid."

"It's not a podium though, is it?"

He had no argument for that. Only the top three got to climb those hallowed steps. They were the only positions that really mattered in racing. Everyone knew that.

"It's only the first race of the season," Charles offered. "You have plenty of time."

Luis relaxed a little. "You're right. I'm too hard on myself. I love to win. What can I say?"

Charles clapped him on the shoulder. "I predict plenty of that in the future. For both of us."

"I hope you're right. Okay, gladiator, go and face your crowd."

South Tel had arranged for a private room in the hotel. Charles really wanted to flop so he thanked his lucky stars he only had to ride the elevator to bed. In days gone by, he would have insisted on finding the most expensive place in town to eat. Now he wanted to curl up under the duvet and sleep. How times had changed.

Luckily, he hadn't come down in his sweatpants and hoodie. The team were packed into the room around a huge table filled with local delicacies. Charles' stomach growled as he took his seat. At the head of the table sat a huge flatscreen TV.

Luis sat with Paulo, who gave Charles another of his nasty scowls. Charles caught his eye and flashed his kilowatt smile. Paulo responded with a bored yawn. The air was so thick he could have cut it with a knife.

"What is his problem?" Will whispered to Charles.

"Not ours to worry about," Charles replied. "Ignore him."

As soon as they'd all settled down, a member of the hotel staff fiddled with a remote control and the screen burst into life to reveal the grinning face of Meera. She had on a South Tel sweatshirt. Even in that, she still looked absolutely stunning. The old Charles would have tried to take their relationship further than boss and driver. Rehab had taught him a lot more about himself than how he would quit booze.

"Ladies and gentlemen," she began, snapping him out of his thoughts. "What can I say? Thank you, all of you, for a wonderful start to the season. A win and fourth place are far more than we hoped for."

All eyes were on Charles. Luis had his head down and Paulo's ever-present evil stare remained firmly fixed on Charles. He had begun to find this really fucking irritating. If Luis thought fourth place a bad result, he would have to get over himself, otherwise the season would be a long one. Besides, Charles didn't feel responsible for Luis' performance. Only his own, and today, that spelt victory.

"Today is only the first step in a very long journey," Meera reminded them. "Don't get complacent. I want it all, remember that."

With a grin, she logged off the Zoom call, leaving the room in silence.

"She doesn't ask for much, does she?" Charles said loudly.

Everyone laughed, the tension from Meera's speech dissolving.

"Meera is a very demanding woman," Barnaby, sitting next to Charles, said. "You're only as good as your last race."

"Anyone for champagne?" Michelle, one of the pit managers, piped up.

The party atmosphere returned to the room, and everyone resumed talking about corners Charles had taken and how quickly they had changed his tyres.

"They're a good team," Charles said, surveying the tables.

"Yeah," Barnaby agreed. "Better than some. Then you are probably best placed to give us a critique."

"I've seen my fair share of drama," Charles replied.

Talk about putting it mildly. Charles had seen it all. He had been a driver for Bodhi Rose a couple of years ago, a midtable team who fought like cat and dog. Even he had tried to suggest to the Team Principal that it wasn't a decent atmosphere to work in. In those days, bars and beer were more important to Charles. Providing the team kept on paying him, he didn't make too many waves.

"I can already tell this is the best move I ever made," he continued.

"Calm down," Will said, swigging from a bottle of beer. "It's only race one."

This time Charles cast a withering glare at his brother. He wouldn't let him ruin this moment. He had a feeling South Tel had the power to take him to the top again where he belonged, and he needed everyone on side for that to happen.

Barnaby stood. "Everyone, before we begin. There's a photographer downstairs."

A few people groaned and made cat calls.

"We don't want a bloody paparazzo in here," Michelle piped up. "We need to relax."

"It's not like that," Barnaby continued. "He's doing a photo report for *The Guardian*. He just needs twenty minutes to get some candid shots. No need for you to pose or anything."

"Is my hair okay?" Charles asked Will, fiddling with his curls.

"You look perfect, stud."

Barnaby took their silence as a yes and nodded to an assistant, who scurried off.

"Is there no bloody peace?" Luis exclaimed, across the table.

"When they have two gorgeous drivers, you can't blame them for wanting to show us off," Charles replied.

Luis smiled. "Maybe you're right."

Charles noticed he also sipped a sparkling water. He had refused the bottle of champagne that Paulo had made light work of. A lot of the younger generation of drivers didn't seem to care for wild partying. Charles might only be Luis' senior by seven years, but he probably looked Jurassic in Luis' eyes.

He might have let the lifestyle overtake him, but he and Will had had some fun over the years.

A beady-eyed man with three cameras slung over his shoulders came into the room. Charles hated photographers. They had caught him in his worst states and splashed them over the tabloids for the world to pick apart over their breakfast.

When he had been good value for them, they had tracked him relentlessly. Another reason why he loved living at Queens Crescent. It was a private road, so they weren't allowed to come onto the street itself. With his house being in the centre, he had been as well protected as possible in a bustling capital city.

"All right, everyone? I'm Frank," he announced. "Thank you for this chance. I won't keep you because I know you're all starving. If you could mill about a bit, that would be great. Luis and Charles, is there any chance of you chatting over by the window? Seems a shame to waste that view."

"So much for real shots," Charles muttered, getting up.

Luis joined him by the window. The view over Bahrain was spectacular. As usual, Charles always regretted not being able to explore the far-flung destinations his career took him to. He rarely got the chance. They were on a flight home before his body clock had even registered the change most of the time.

"I would have worn something a bit fancier if I'd known," Luis said.

"I nearly came in my pyjamas," Charles replied.

Luis frowned. "You wear pyjamas?"

"Only when I'm alone."

The flash lit up the room and Charles gave his winning smile, a smile that had earnt him almost as much in sponsorship deals as his driving skills had. He had contracts with a flashy watch manufacturer, a clothing line, and an online betting app. To his amazement, they had stuck with him through his recent troubles...albeit at a very reduced rate.

"Okay, if you could just chat to each other for ten minutes," Frank said, "I'll get some shots and leave you be."

Paulo instantly appeared at Luis' side. "We didn't approve this," he said. "I don't like it."

"Ah, relax," Will said, also joining them. "It's no big deal."

Paulo scowled at him. He really did have a face that would sour milk. Charles couldn't understand why a seemingly sweet guy like Luis needed this man in his life. Luis' sexuality had been public knowledge for years. Charles wondered if there was more to this relationship than met the eye. And why did he find himself caring so much?

"We'll get the main course out of the way then make our excuses," Paulo continued, totally ignoring Will.

"Luis," Charles said. "I know you're annoyed with yourself

for today. A fourth place is not something to be upset about. You'll have plenty of chances to get on that podium."

He had meant it to sound encouraging but feared it came across patronising.

"At your age, I'm surprised you could even climb on it," Paulo muttered.

"What did you just say?" Will growled, his whole body going rigid.

"It's fine," Charles said, placing a guiding hand on Will's shoulder. "I didn't mean anything by it, Paulo. I don't like to see anyone beating themselves up for no reason."

Luis glanced from one to the other, staying maddeningly quiet.

"I suppose we should be grateful you're even standing," Paulo continued.

Will had clearly had enough and launched himself at the younger man. Will had always been built like the proverbial outhouse, a diet of rugby and weights from an early age giving him a solid body. The slight Paulo stood no chance and in no time found himself up against the window with Will's face right next to his own.

"Will. No," Charles shouted, grabbing hold of his brother's shirt.

"You need to keep your vicious little tongue in check," Will snarled. "The bitchy queen act gets stale very quickly."

With all his strength, Charles hauled Will off Paulo.

"That's right, Worthington.," Paulo sneered. "Drag your ape to his cage."

Will made another attempt for Paulo, but Charles stopped him. "I'll go for you myself if you don't shut the fuck up," Charles said to Paulo before turning to Luis. "Are you going to put up with this?"

Luis had gone bright red. "Paulo. Be quiet."

It was like throwing a pint pot of water on a raging bush fire.

Paulo rearranged his shirt and grinned. He clearly enjoyed getting a rise out of people.

"Of course. My apologies if my truth hurts. That's more on you, isn't it? How many people fail after rehab? I can't remember the statistics."

This time, Charles had had enough, and he lunged for Paulo. Luis stood in his way and they both tumbled to the floor. They weren't fighting as such. Charles shoved him away and got to his feet, his night of victory crumbling around his ears.

"What on earth is going on?" Barnaby raged. "Oh shit."

They all followed his gaze to see the photographer beating a hasty retreat. No doubt his payday for a boring behind-the-scenes reportage had been replaced by a much bigger prize.

"For fuck's sake," Charles roared.

CHAPTER FOUR

Two days later and Charles sat in his kitchen, staring for the umpteenth time at the headlines from the day before.

War on the track, screamed one.

Fight for supremacy, said another.

Worthington on the floor, again, said a third.

They were all accompanied by photos of him and Luis rolling around. The photographer would most likely be sitting on a beach somewhere now. Charles didn't even blame him. They all operated in a dog-eat-dog world, and Luis and Charles had thrown him the biggest bone.

He got up, unable to read them again. His long-suffering PR agent, Hilary Milligan, had done a decent damage control exercise. The day before he'd appeared on *Breakfast Britain* to explain how the photo had been a moment in time, unfairly capitalised on.

Luis had done the same with some of the red-top papers. Now they had to hope it would be a storm in a teacup. The newspapers loved a bitter rivalry. They would be upset their favourite drunk had reformed and would be praying for a relapse. Charles could handle that. He hated the idea of unsettling the team after such a powerful beginning. Meera had made it perfectly clear she would not tolerate shit from either of them. Plus, the work he'd done to get Barnaby on side had evaporated like mist.

The doorbell rang through the house, making him jump. On his way, he checked his reflection in the hall mirror. *Not bad.* His smart but casual outfit of a dusky pink cashmere sweater and white jeans made him come across as healthy and tan.

Taking a deep breath, he opened the door. "Well, hello," he said with a beam.

"Hello, Charles," Luis replied.

"Come on in."

He ushered Luis into the house. Glancing down to the main road, all was quiet. *Typical—the paparazzi are never there when you need them.* A few long-range shots wouldn't have gone astray. He'd half expected Hilary to tip them off when he told her his plans..

As they walked into the kitchen, Luis winced at the newspapers all spread out on the kitchen table. "We made a pig's ear of that, didn't we?" he asked.

"Here," Charles said, taking Luis' jacket. "You could say that. What can I get you?"

Luis sank down on one of the metal chairs that the shop had convinced Charles had an industrial Bauhaus vibe. They were in fact simply uncomfortable.

"I'll have a coffee," Luis replied, frowning at one of the headlines.

Charles fired up the coffee maker. Something about Luis made him so uncomfortable he was glad of something to do. "You come off better than me," Charles said, over his shoulder. "I'm the big bad wolf that floored the innocent pup."

Luis sighed. "I'm sorry. It was supposed to be your moment of glory."

Leaning against the kitchen counter, Charles studied his face. He was so handsome. Even more so in the flesh, which often wasn't the case. The decency that shone out of him made him special.

"That's okay," he replied. "I'll just have to make sure there's plenty more. We both will, otherwise Meena will have our balls for a charm bracelet."

"She has a lot of money on us," Luis mused. "So, if we don't perform, I suppose that's the least she can expect."

Charles might be happy to provide Meera with some podium wins, but he drew the line at his genitals. The coffee machine beeped that the espressos were ready. Charles put one down in front of Luis and took a seat.

"Thank you for the invitation," Luis said.

He spoke in a slow drawl, as if he considered every word he spoke carefully. After spending most of his days with Will who had absolutely no filter, Charles found it comforting.

"You're welcome," he beamed. "I'm no cook, so it's pasta. You're not vegetarian, are you? Shit, I should have asked."

"No, I'm not vegetarian."

"Phew," Charles said. He hated cooking in front of people. If he entertained, he usually got caterers in. Today he'd wanted to at least try to impress Luis. So, he'd made (in truth Will had done most of the heavy lifting) cannelloni. Not very original but safe.

"Are you okay?" Luis asked.

Charles sighed. "Sorry. I'm a bit nervous, I guess."

The laughter that came from Luis made Charles jump. "What?" He frowned.

"You're Charles Worthington," Luis explained. "Nothing gets to you. I've watched you swagger around the world for fifteen years."

He didn't know if Luis was mocking him or not. He didn't like it. "I'm not sure if you got the memo," he muttered. "There's new management in town."

The jovial expression dropped from Luis' face. "I'm sorry,

Charles. I didn't mean to laugh. Of course I know how the last few years have been for you. Damn, we seem to have a habit of saying the wrong things."

He sipped his coffee thoughtfully. Charles breathed a sigh of relief that he didn't grimace after.

"I think we're being too careful around each other," Charles declared.

"Too careful?" Luis replied, shocked.

"Yes," Charles continued. "I really want this to work. Meera and Barnaby have taken a chance on me, and I want to repay them. You have contract negotiations this year."

He noticed Luis bristle at this, but it wasn't a secret.

"And you think we're trying to be sickly sweet to make it happen?" Luis considered this. "Well, we've made a right fuck-up of that."

The joke relaxed them both. Charles hadn't expected Luis to have a potty mouth. Everything else about him seemed so angelic.

"Tell me three facts about you that nobody knows," Charles said, eager to delve deeper.

Luis groaned. "Really?"

"Go on. We did this at rehab and when you're in the public eye, it's bloody harder than it looks."

Luis sat back and scrunched his eyes up as he thought. It gave Charles a chance to watch him. He had an almost innocent face, stunning complexion, and jet-black hair. They couldn't be more opposite if they tried.

"Okay," Luis said suddenly, making Charles jump. "You ready?"

Charles grinned. "I was born ready."

Luis raised an eyebrow. "You were born corny, you mean."

Waving him away, Charles wanted some little-known facts about this man. His interest was piqued now. "Go on."

"Right," Luis said, rubbing his hands together. "Number

one, I must have two fried eggs and wholemeal toast before a race. Two, I have a tattoo of a chequered flag. Three, my thumb is double jointed."

He held it up proudly and jiggled it, so it seemed to fall in and out of the socket.

"And where is this tattoo?" Charles asked.

"Ah, that's a fourth fact and you only asked for three," Luis said with a smile. "Your go."

Charles thought about the stock answers he'd given in rehab. He wanted to make this more meaningful than that. "Okay, first I have to sleep on the right side of the bed with my right leg out of the covers. Two, my favourite cheese is Roquefort. Three, I think I'm probably gay."

That made Luis' mouth drop open, causing Charles to crease up. He had absolutely no idea why he'd trusted Luis with that most personal of secrets. Something about him made Charles want to open up. His stock third fact was that he had blocked up Elton John's toilet, which had raised a laugh or two in group therapy. That moment had long since passed.

"Charles..."

Charles held his hand up. "Nope, I don't wish to discuss it. I'm just getting used to saying it."

He leapt up to prepare things. The oven timer told him he had seconds to go. Luis being in his kitchen made him nervous, something he hadn't prepared himself for. With the brief respite, he focused on lowering his heart rate. He'd just told someone who wasn't a paid professional or family member his deepest secret. Surprisingly, the world hadn't exploded on impact.

He dished up the food. All the while, Luis hadn't stopped watching him. Self-consciously he put the plates down.

"Dig in," he said. "It's nothing special."

"I disagree. This is wonderful," Luis said, spearing a cucumber piece. "And all very much on our diet sheets."

Charles shook his head. "Dr Evil, the nutritionist, has my fridge bugged, I swear it."

They ate in silence for a minute or two before Luis regarded him. "You know I'm going to ask."

Charles sighed. "Can't we forget I said anything? Fuck knows why I did."

Once again, Luis considered his words carefully before he spoke. How did he do that? Charles suspected he had been trained by Meera. "I think because you wanted to talk about it with me."

Perhaps he had a point. Luis had never made a secret of his sexuality. There had been no grand coming out and heart-wrenching book. He'd just never hidden it.

"You're the future for gay people," Charles said. "I admire that."

Shrugging, Luis carried on with his meal. "I don't see what's to admire. I'm just me."

"You're kidding, right?" Charles said. "You showed anyone like...us, well, that it can be done."

Luis had been a revelation to the gay community. He graced billboards and had a ton of contracts to his name. In the alpha-male world of Formula One, he'd beaten a new path, perhaps contributing in no small way to Charles finally feeling brave enough to be honest about himself.

"That isn't to say people don't want me to fail," Luis replied. "Diego, who did Meera's job before her? He hated me. If he couldn't take a driver out to a strip club, he had no idea how to bond with them."

"Fucking dinosaur," Charles muttered. He thought it prudent not to mention the countless visits to strip clubs he'd had with Diego Sanchez over the years.

"Anyway, nice try at deflection," Luis said, putting his fork down and staring at Charles. "How the fuck can Charles

Worthington, the man who views Fashion Week as his own personal Tinder, be gay?"

He had opened this can of worms so he could hardly blame Luis for wanting to know the full story. At rehab they had told him it was good to share. Perhaps this time he'd jumped in where he shouldn't have done. "If I talk to you about this, I need to know it remains between us."

"Of course."

"I mean it," he urged. "I don't want your vicious little bodyguard getting wind of it."

Luis shifted uncomfortably in his seat. "Paulo is okay. You got off to a bad start with him. He's very protective."

So were Rottweilers. "That's my point. If he gets hold of something to use against me... I hate to tell you this, but he bloody well will."

"I agree," Luis said. "He won't hear anything from me."

"What's the deal with you two? Sleeping together?"

"More deflection, Worthington. Speak."

Something deep within him told him to trust Luis Salvatore. "Okay, I did a lot of soul searching in rehab," Charles said. "I've always been bi. I never made a big deal of it. Now I think, in reality, I'm gay. Which is going to come as a shock to a lot of women if I ever go public."

Luis chewed thoughtfully. "And will you?"

"Go public?"

The million-dollar question that Charles had thought long and hard about. Ultimately that had to be the goal. He only had a few years left in Formula One. So, he'd made the decision to wait until he hung up his racing gloves. Any damage from the fallout would be far less. If need be, Charles had planned to step out of the public eye. After fifteen years, the sheen had gone from that life anyway.

"I don't think so. Not for the foreseeable," he replied. "It's no fucker's business."

"The press might have something to say about that."

The newspapers were the bane of his life. "They're too busy inventing you and me taking pot shots at each other," Charles said.

"I don't like that," Luis replied. "It's distracting."

Charles nodded in agreement. If people thought they were warring, they wouldn't support the team. No one liked bad sportsmanship.

The rest of lunch passed in an easy conversation about everything from the pit crew to the tyres to their favourite racetracks.

When it came time for Luis to go, Charles found himself wishing the night could go on forever. He nearly suggested going to a bar. He chickened out in case it gave off the wrong impression. Besides, Luis was so sure of himself and for once, Charles wasn't. Something he did not like one bit.

"What you up to tonight?" he asked.

"Paulo is coming over," Luis said. "We're doing movies and nachos."

"Sounds fun."

Luis shrugged. "Not up to your standard, but we like it."

Walking him to the door, Charles realised that the party-boy image he'd spent years cultivating had turned into a prison cell. And that any hope of escape would take more digging than *The Shawshank Redemption*.

"I enjoyed today, Charles," Luis said.

"I did too," Charles replied. "Look at us. Sober as judges too."

Luis placed his hand on his Charles' shoulder, the heat from his hand making Charles groin twitch alarmingly. "You don't have to get shitfaced to have fun."

The words seemed loaded. Didn't they? "Some fun is better sober," Charles replied, in an equally loaded tone.

Luis held his gaze for a second longer than was strictly

comfortable. They walked down Charles' steps and over to Luis' car.

"I'll see you on the plane then," Charles said. "I think we should make a big show of travelling together."

"Yes, Barnaby will be pleased, if nothing else."

Once more, Luis shot him that quizzical look before getting into his car. Revving the engine, he wound the window down. "See you," he said.

Charles nodded as Luis accelerated out of the Crescent.

"What an attractive young man."

Whirling round, Charles came face to face with Mrs Wimpole, Queens Crescent matriarch and keeper of secrets. She lived slap bang in the centre of Queens Crescent and had done since God was a boy. She viewed the area as her personal fiefdom, and nothing went on without her knowledge. "Yes, I suppose he is."

A glint in Mrs Wimpole's eye suggested she wouldn't be fooled that easily. "And is he a friend of yours? I must say, I'm very relieved that we don't have a different dollybird parading up and down the Crescent every week."

Mrs Wimpole didn't mince her words. They made him wince at times. He respected her for such honesty though. A rarity in his world.

"Ah, Mrs W, I'm done with all that now," Charles said.

She patted him on the arm. "Well done. I've been monitoring your progress. I think a nice, sensible friend is what you need now. I wish you all the luck."

With that, she pottered off, probably to accost another neighbour. Charles watched her retreat.

A friend like him is exactly what I need.

CHAPTER FIVE

The next day, Charles found himself in Meera's glass office. It overlooked the main floor where she had a vantage point over her world.

"It was a good win," she said.

She had dressed for the part in a black tailored suit and striped shirt. Settling in her chair, she absentmindedly played with a pen as she focused in on him.

"Thank you," he replied.

It had felt a bit like being summoned to the head teacher's office when he'd got the call that morning to come over within the hour.

"So, what the fuck happened after?"

It had been expected. She didn't seem to the type to summon a driver to discuss the finer points of taking corners over a pot of tea.

"Honestly, Meera. A misunderstanding has been blown up out of all proportion," Charles said. "My brother and Will were arguing. Luis and I simply stepped in. We were trying to avoid trouble if anything."

Throwing the pen onto the desk, she got up and stalked over

to the window. Charles had always been a confident person, but Meera unsettled him.

"I will not have the press inventing a war within my team. Do you hear me?"

As a new entrant to this world, Charles would play along so far. He would not be dragged across London on his day off to be spoken to like a child.

"Then you should speak to your PR person about that," he muttered. "Next time that jumped-up little fuck Paulo pushes my brother over the edge, I'll let him kick the shit out of him. You have my word."

A smile crept onto Meera's face. "It probably wouldn't do him any harm to get a beating, but you need to muzzle your brother, or I'll be forced to ban them both."

Now it was time for Charles to get up and walk over to the glass window. He could just imagine the power Meera felt as she stood in her eyrie, watching her minions working away below. He needed her on side. No matter what Barnaby, Luis, or even sleazy Paulo thought, if he had Meera, he had the team.

"I really am sorry," he said in his sexiest voice.

She sighed and moved away from him.

"I truly hope you aren't going to try that," she replied. "My husband is ten times sexier than you. Besides, my sources tell me I'm not your type these days."

Luis.

"What?" Charles asked, floored by her directness.

"I have a lot of people telling me a lot of things, Mr Worthington," she said with a knowing smile. "Not a lot gets past me."

The room had become hot, making him clammy. It was his tell when he got stressed, and he hated it. "Whatever I do in my private life is none of your business," he snapped.

"Correct," she replied. "Providing you don't bring it to work.

Brawling in full view of a photographer with your teammate is doing just that."

He had had enough of this. "On the back of the first win of the season," he barked back. "If you hauled me in here to give me a warning, consider it done. I trust I can go now?"

"Not quite," Meera said. "There's a premiere tonight. Bond. Nice and alpha male. You and Luis are going."

"What?" Charles said. "It's the night before we fly to Monaco. I had plans."

"That you will cancel," she replied. "I want it in all the papers before you set foot on that jet tomorrow. I believe my PR man lives on the same street as you. Nihal Varma?"

Charles knew him well. Nihal had been trying to get Charles as a client for years, but Charles had been with Hilary Milligan since the beginning though. An old-school, hard-nosed PR woman, she struck fear into the heart of Fleet Street. Hilary would probably want him hung, drawn, and quartered if she heard he had attended a Varma event. Unfortunately for Hilary, he feared her marginally less than Meera.

"Fine," he said. "Who told you about me?"

"You don't need to know about that," Meera said, sitting down. "I've been hard on you today and I realise it. I won't punish you for who you are, Charles. I also won't have it affect your performance. Do we have an understanding?"

Charles shrugged. "I'll prove to you I can be consistent."

When he got home, he was seriously pissed off. Will sat in the first-floor lounge, watching some mindless crap on the television.

"Get your fucking feet off the couch," Charles demanded.

Sitting up, Will scowled. "You're not going to have another bloody go at me, are you?"

Charles flopped down in his favourite chair by the window. What he wouldn't give for a slug of vodka right now. "I got hauled over red-hot coals by bloody Meera because of your scrapping," he replied. "Is there a chance you're going to behave yourself going forward?"

To his credit, Will seemed embarrassed. "I'll apologise to Luis."

"And Paulo."

"Oh, for fuck's sake," Will muttered. He stopped when he registered the withering glance from Charles. "Fine, and Paulo."

"She knows about me as well."

"What about you?"

"About me being gay."

It had been a hard moment when he'd had to tell Will the truth about himself. For years, they had been wingmen. The Worthington brothers partied with the best of them. Women flocked to them.

At first Will had thought him coming out to be the product of rehab. He accused Charles of trying to find a reason for his addiction. Charles' bisexuality had been an open secret for years, but for him to renounce their years of pursuit of the opposite sex had threatened their very relationship.

"How?" Will said. "That's none of her fucking business."

Good old Will. Their sibling bond had prevailed and now he protected Charles as fiercely as ever.

"It kind of becomes her business when you are pictured brawling with the only openly gay driver's assistant."

"Back to me again," Will grumbled. "Why didn't she call me in then?"

"Because you're not on her payroll, dickhead," Charles said. "If you carry on, she'll ban you, and there isn't anything I can do about it."

Narrowing his eyes, Will regarded his brother. "I hope she isn't blackmailing you."

Poor Will did live in the nineties sometimes.

"No, brother. It was an aside, although I'd like to know where she found out. I suppose Luis."

"You told him?"

"It just came out."

"As did you," Will replied. "Little fuck."

In his heart, Charles couldn't believe that Luis had sold him out to Meera. He had come across as so genuine and decent. He kicked his brogues off and wriggled his toes.

"I've hardly been a monk since I got out of rehab," he said. "It might be any of the guys from Grindr."

He had gone a bit crazy recently. Ever the addictive personality, he had swapped shots for cocks and a very nice time he'd had too.

"Anyway, I've got to go to a bloody premiere tonight with Luis. Bond, so it's nice and manly."

Will chuckled. "Not a date then."

"God no," Charles said, a little too quickly.

Once again, his brother studied him. "But you'd like it to be."

"I don't know," Charles said. "There's something about him."

Will shook his head. "Bad move, big bro. Very bad move."

"My favourite kind," Charles replied with a glint in his eye.

"I'm not getting involved," Will said. "I get into enough trouble on my own, thanks."

"Ain't that the truth. Right, move your lardy arse—we're going to Grizedale's," Charles said, getting up. "I've got a fitting."

Will leapt to his feet. "I might get something myself."

Charles clapped him on the shoulder. "On my account, no doubt."

Kissing his cheek, Will ruffled his hair. "That's what big brothers are for."

Laughing, they threw their coats on and made their way down the outside steps and onto Queens Crescent. As they passed Mrs Wimpole's, Charles saw her in her usual spot by the window. He gave her a cheery wave, which she returned.

"She never misses a bloody trick," Will said.

"No one will lie dead in their house for long on Queens Crescent," Charles said. "Mrs Wimpole would have us chipped if she thought she'd get away with it."

Queens Parade was a small row of shops that lay a little way off the main street. The burdens of modernity had pretty much left it alone. There were no chains here. The Queens Parade Conservation Society wouldn't allow it.

Charles pretended he didn't care about things like that but secretly he loved it. To be able to shop in places that everyone else didn't was a luxury only couture generally offered. Not that Charles was averse to spending a small fortune in Knightsbridge. There had to be some spoils for all his hard work.

Anthony Grizedale had been the local tailor in the row of shops since around the time Charles moved to the area. They had struck up a friendship almost immediately. One drunken night it had been a little more than that. Charles hadn't been ready and Anthony hadn't really been that interested.

"Charlie boy," Anthony exclaimed. "And he's brought his big Willy."

Will rolled his eyes. "That gets funnier every time, Tony."

Anthony swatted him over the head with a tape measure. "Never Tony. Ant I can forgive but Tony makes me sound like a cab driver."

"Imagine," Charles said, drily. "I got your email. The suit is ready?"

"Ah yes. I'll go and get it. We need to check it for any alterations."

Anthony disappeared into the storeroom. Charles occupied himself by examining the ties. He had never really been into major formal attire. He found it far too restrictive. Give him a race suit any day. His mind strayed to Luis in his tight race suit. How could a man focus when that was being paraded in front of him almost daily?

He had noticed that Luis' suit fitted him far more snugly than Charles'. Perhaps Paulo had paid the designers a little extra to show off the Salvatore curves. Charles wouldn't put anything past that little snake.

Will held up some cufflinks. "These are nice."

Charles shook his head. He never stayed mad at his brother for long. "Fine," he said. "Add them to your collection."

Doing a little dance, Will put them on the shop counter.

"Another gift for Willy?" Anthony asked as he bustled through.

"A bonus, actually," Will replied. "For all my hard work."

Anthony stared over his glasses at Will. "Brawling in public? I'd love to see your job description."

Charles took the suit from Anthony's outstretched hand and headed for the fitting room. "Less said about that, the better, Ant," he called over his shoulder. "Still a bit of a sore point."

He drew the curtain and started to take off his clothes. "If it fits, can I have it tonight?"

"Bloody hell, Charles," Anthony replied. "You must have fifty suits at home. Why do you want it so quickly?"

"He has a date," Will chimed in.

He grimaced as he put the suit on. Charles had absolutely no doubt it would fit. Anthony had been dressing him for over a decade and he got the sizes right first time. They had to do this little ritual every time, to make Anthony feel he was going the extra mile.

Anthony also thrived on gossip. To be fair to him, he kept most things to himself and had been a source of support to Charles. Charles had some good people in his life, something he felt inordinately lucky about.

"A date?" Anthony exclaimed. "You've been a little quiet on that front recently. Who's the lucky lady?"

Charles caught his reflection in the mirror. While he might be open to his nearest and dearest, that was a long way away from the world knowing. He hated living a lie, but a lot of money rested on his reputation.

A dabble in bisexuality could be explained away as bohemian. Major sponsors would have a problem with a seismic change in sexuality.

"It's Luis Salvatore," Charles shouted through. "And it's a work thing."

He buttoned up the jacket and stepped through the curtain to see an amused Will and Anthony looking at him.

"What?" he asked.

"A work thing?" Anthony sighed. "Well, I suppose the customer is always right."

To his credit, Will didn't back him up. Charles would have killed him if he gave the baseless rumour mongering any credence. He might be a wind-up merchant, but he also knew that Charles needed to be in charge of his own life.

"You look killer, big bro," Will said, mercifully changing the subject.

"Yes, I like it," he said, checking himself out in the big mirror.

The suit was jet black. He had wanted it to be as matt as possible. It would work so well against the glare of photographer's flashbulbs. It had originally been intended for an awards dinner, but he didn't see any reason why it couldn't have its maiden voyage that night.

Who am I kidding? There's only one reason I want to look hot tonight.

CHAPTER SIX

Four hours later and he and Luis were in a limo on the way to Leicester Square. Luis rocked a tuxedo like Bond himself. Charles hadn't scrubbed up badly either.

"Did Meera drag you into the office?" Charles asked.

The streets of London passed by, filled with workers and tourists. Most of them went about their business while a few tried to peer into the car window to see who sat behind the smoked glass.

"Yes," Luis replied. "She can be quite the tyrant when she wants to be."

Charles grinned at him. "I guess her two drivers scrapping isn't an everyday occurrence."

Luis caught his eye, shaking his head. "Nor will it be."

"Fair enough," Charles said.

They sat in silence for a while. The traffic had blocked every road as other cars tried to edge their way onto the iconic little square which housed every premiere going. Adding into the mix royalty would be attending and they had all the ingredients of a major event—something the twisty little streets of London had not been designed for all those centuries ago.

"This is ridiculous," Luis said. "Shall we just walk?"

As fast car drivers, nothing annoyed them more than traffic jams. Charles knew exactly where Luis was coming from. Even if he was a passenger, it still wound hm up. "Fine, come on," he agreed.

"We'll walk," Luis shouted through to the driver.

Once out on the street, a few people excitedly pointed. Charles put his head down and walked towards the cinemas. They were only a few streets away.

"Hey, wait," Luis said, catching up with him. "What's up with you?"

"They all recognised us," Charles said, taking a left.

"And?"

"You never know who's around," Charles replied. "Keep close to me."

As they found their way onto the square, people jostled for position to see the next celebrity to go in. Screams erupted here and there when people saw their favourites. Charles had never really understood the world of famous people. Nowadays, people finding fame just for fame's sake twisted his mind even more.

"Fuck," Charles complained.

Luis took hold of Charles' hand, the touch making him gasp.

"What are you doing?" he asked.

"Don't be so soft," Luis said. "Do you want to get separated?"

As though it were the most natural thing in the world, Luis led him through the crowds. They moved fast with their heads down. By the time people had recognised them and they heard their names, they were way in front. By the time they got to the Odeon Cinema, Charles was out of breath. Luis dropped his hand and Charles found himself missing his touch.

"Wow, you can move," Charles said.

"You'd better believe it," Luis replied, with a wink.

Another loaded statement. Luis Salvatore confused Charles. Charles liked it.

An official guarded the end of the red carpet. She ushered them through when they produced their golden tickets.

"Ready?" Charles asked Luis.

Luis frowned, glancing at the huge pack of photographers and fans. "It's pretty fucking big," he replied.

"Come on," Charles said. He took hold of Luis' hand, and this time, he led Luis past the barriers and onto the red carpet. The crowds were screaming, and the photographers were shouting so many different names that they had no idea which way to look.

Luckily, Charles was no stranger to this rodeo, and he posed expertly. Poor Luis seemed as though he wanted the ground to open and swallow him whole. He stood rigid with an expression that looked like he was passing wind rather than at the movie of the year.

"Not your scene?" Charles grinned.

"God, no," Luis replied, grimacing. "What a fucking nightmare."

"Try and appear you're having a good time," Charles whispered.

Luis attempted the worst fake smile Charles had ever seen.

"I think we need to work on this," he chuckled.

Luis stuck his tongue out. The cameras flashed all the more.

"Fucking hell," Luis whispered. "I suppose that will go bloody viral."

"That's the world we're living in, baby," Charles replied. "Watch."

He placed one foot in front of the other, his hand casually in his trouser pocket, and flashed his pearly white teeth. The place lit up and the photographers shouted his name.

"Come on," Charles urged through gritted teeth.

Luis sighed and copied him but a mirror image. The photographers were going crazy for a shot of the new teammates and supposed rivals. A few tried to throw some questions out there. Charles and Luis just ignored them. They were photos-only that night.

"Now that'll be everywhere," Charles said.

"Thank you," Luis replied. "This is so not my game."

The movie star and Charles' neighbour, Madeline Morrison, was ahead of them. She had a minor role in this movie and had adopted the air of main star. She took ages answering every question and posing from all angles. Madeline seemed completely oblivious she had caused a major gridlock on the queue. Or perhaps she just didn't care.

"Ah, Charles," she said as they air kissed. "And Luis Salvatore. What a delicious duo."

Charles shrugged. "South Tel's best, Madeline."

Madeline scanned Luis like a cat watches an oblivious little mouse. Charles found himself standing in between them.

Why the fuck am I getting all protective?

"Of course," she replied. "I guess it doesn't matter if you win or lose. You're the hottest team this season."

"We will tell Meera," Luis said with a remarkably straight face.

Charles imagined how that would go down.

Madeline didn't grace him with a response as she resumed her glide down the carpet. She deigned to sign the odd autograph on her way but kept her eye firmly on the end goal...the free bar.

"You know what, you're right," Charles said. "This shit is stale sober."

Charles and Luis were a little more gracious than Madeline, however. They signed autographs, posed for seemingly endless selfies and chatted with fans. Charles noticed that Luis suddenly came alive. He genuinely vibed from talking to people. Following his lead, Charles joked with the crowd who lapped it up.

Nihal Varma was standing in the doorway by the time they got there. Varma was an incredibly handsome man. Charles had secretly lusted after him for years, but even he knew that sleeping with his PR guru neighbour wouldn't be wise. He might as well tell Mrs Wimpole he liked boys and be done with it.

"Charles Worthington," Nihal said, giving Charles a hug. "It must be nice for you to come to a professionally run event. Do let Hilary know what it's like."

Charles wagged his finger at Nihal. "Play nice, Mr V," he said. "Or she'll eat you for breakfast."

They walked over the threshold of the iconic cinema like so many other stars had done before. Even though he had been in this game for fifteen years, Charles struggled with being famous. It had so many positives. The negatives, however, were brutal.

Many of his school friends from the criminally expensive private school his parents had sent him to had made it into the public eye. Even so, Charles had only ever wanted to race. The rest of it had taken over and dragged him to a place he never wanted to return to.

"Do we have to stay for the film?" Luis said. "We could escape out of the back. We've done what Meera wanted."

"Not a fan of Bond?" Charles asked.

"Not a fan of late nights when I'm racing in a few days," Luis replied. "Neither should you be."

Charles shrugged. "If you hadn't leapt on me in front of that photographer, we wouldn't be in this position."

Luis opened his mouth to argue when he must have seen the glint in Charles' eye. "You're taking the piss?" he asked.

"Yup." Charles chuckled. "I do that a lot."

"I am getting that impression."

Inside, the bar area seemed to contain every face from the

supermarket scandal sheets. Charles waved at a few people he had partied way too hard with over the years. The usual suspects were there, B list actors, reality stars, and a gaggle of people Charles had no idea about.

"Who the fuck are they?" He frowned.

"Ah, poor old man," Luis teased. "That's the YouTube army. Don't you keep up?"

Charles shoved him gently. "Drink?" he asked.

Luis nodded. He had relaxed marginally inside the building but still gave off major fish-out-of-water vibes.

Once Charles fought his way to the bar, he would have given his right testicle for a shot of vodka. Instead, he ordered a sparkling water. "What do you want?"

"Same as you," Luis replied.

"You can have something stronger, you know. It doesn't bother me."

"I would never do that to you."

The way that Luis said that made Charles' heart dance. Even Will had no worries about drinking beer in his house, even if he made sure not to leave any. The fact that Luis, someone he barely knew, would make that concession for him touched Charles.

Armed with two waters, they found a perch on a step behind a huge cardboard cut-out of the latest Bond.

"You look better than him," Charles chuckled. "I'll give you your due, you know how to pull off a tuxedo. Not everyone can manage it."

As if on cue, a rather portly celebrity best known for his appearances in panto walked past. He had on a threadbare dinner suit and garish pink cummerbund.

"I rest my case," Charles whispered.

They burst into fits of giggles.

"I needed that," Luis said. "It's intense out there."

They watched a few scantily clad women clattering past in heels and screeching with laughter at something.

"They must be cold," Luis observed.

He had an innocence about him that made Charles want to shield him from this cruel world of headlines and exclusives. No wonder he had rejected the celebrity life. He wouldn't last five minutes. It might seem like the ultimate goal to outsiders, but as a casualty, Charles had had more than his fair share of the pitfalls of fame. He had learnt the hard way.

"What do you do for fun?" Charles asked. He found he wanted to know everything about this new person that had been shoved into his life.

"My foundation keeps me busy," Luis replied. "I like to read or cook. I'm really quite boring."

Staring into those stunning blue eyes, Charles grinned. "I think you're anything but boring." Charles felt he were living in a cliché at that moment. It was as though everything else fell away and he solely focused on Luis.

"Do you?" Luis replied. "I would have thought the great Charles Worthington would have a gang of interesting people."

He had been one of the most popular people on the circuit. They had all disappeared when he had fallen into difficulties. He'd even spotted some in the bar only feet away. No doubt they would make a fuss and promise to catch up. Charles could see through it all now.

"You know, only Will was there for me when I came out of rehab," Charles said. "All this. It's just bullshit."

Luis watched the endless parade of people. "It doesn't surprise me," he replied. "That's why I never wanted a part of it."

Every fibre of Charles wanted to kiss him right then and there. He could just imagine Meera's reaction to that, let alone Luis'. She had wanted to kill a rivalry. He didn't think she would be too pleased at swapping it for an ill-conceived kiss in front of the world's press. "You're a revelation, Luis Salvatore," he said, instead.

Luis caught his eye. "So are you," he smiled. "This season is going to be an interesting one."

Charles leant against Luis. "Who knows where it will take us."

They stared into each other's eyes as though a connection had been made. What type of connection, Charles had no idea.

"I..." Charles began.

"Ladies and gentlemen, please take your seats," came the voice from the Tannoy.

The moment was spectacularly broken, and Charles got to his feet. "We'd better go in."

"What were you going to say then?" Luis asked.

"Don't worry about it," Charles replied gruffly.

The world had come rushing in. Getting entangled with Luis would only be a huge mistake. A quick tumble and they would hate each other for the rest of the season. It would inevitably be his fault for corrupting poor innocent Luis. Charles had no intention of being on Meera's hitlist again.

"Charlie."

Supermodel Jeannie Butler dashed across the lobby toward them. She had on a chainmail tunic dress that left very little to the imagination. Not that Charles needed to use it—they had been an item for six months a few years previously. She was a decent kid.

"Jeannie," he said, kissing her on the cheek. "How are you doing?"

"Is it really five years since we set that red carpet ablaze at the last Bond do?" Jeannie asked in her trademark northern accent.

They had been on all the social pages. Jeannie had upstaged the latest Bond girl by wearing a dress with logos cut out in strategic places. Charles had worn a bright pink tuxedo.

As he hugged her, he saw Luis over her shoulder, scowling. "Jeannie," he said, "have you met my new teammate, Luis Salvatore?"

Jeannie gave him her front-page smile. "It's easier to keep up with Charles' girlfriends than teammates," she smiled. "Pleased to meet you."

"And you," Luis replied brusquely.

If Jeannie had been shaken or stirred by his reaction, she didn't show it. Charles wondered what made Luis be so rude. From what Charles had seen of his teammate, it went completely against his personality.

"It was lovely to see you. Enjoy the movie," she said breezily and skipped off.

"What is your problem?" Charles asked.

"Me?" Luis replied. "No issues. I'm going to bail. Are you coming?"

Charles shook his head. "I'm a sucker for a Bond movie."

"Fine," Luis said and set off towards the rear entrance. A lot of stars used that entrance when they were only interested in the red-carpet photo opportunity. It seemed Luis would do his duty. No more, no less.

Charles watched him go. This season was most certainly going to be an interesting one.

CHAPTER SEVEN

It had been quite the atmosphere in the South Tel private jet on the way over to Monaco. Whether by design or by accident, Barnaby had arranged for it to be just Charles, Luis, Will Paulo, and himself.

To everyone's credit, they had shared the space with no major issue. Will had done the decent thing and apologised to Paulo. Charles noticed that Paulo had merely accepted it and not reciprocated. He hoped that hadn't been lost on the Team Principal too.

Someone as seasoned as Barnaby must have the measure of Paulo. Although, Charles found it hard to decipher if Paulo were in love with Luis or the lifestyle.

Then he stared at Will. He had been with him through thick and thin. Perhaps Paulo was simply an overprotective friend. Charles had been stung by his share of fair-weather friends over the years. It had made him wary and cynical. Not a good look.

His gaze rested on Luis. He had kept out of that fake world so well it was remarkable. Such strength of character astounded Charles. That had been an area he had failed in spectacularly over the years.

Luis caught his eye and glanced away. They hadn't really spoken much. Charles still wanted to know why Luis had suddenly stormed out of the cinema. He wasn't about to have that conversation with Will, Paulo, and Barnaby listening in though.

"Gentlemen, we are about fifteen minutes from landing," the cabin crew member said.

"We'll buckle up," Charles said with his best smouldering smirk.

She returned that grin and went back into the staff area.

"Another one of your conquests?" Paulo asked. "Or simply the next one?"

"Paulo," Luis interjected, glancing at Barnaby who seemed lost in a magazine. "If you get a slap again, I'm not stepping in. Remember that."

Paulo scowled. "I didn't mean anything by it. Everyone knows he's a shagging machine."

"Looks to me like you could do with a bit," Will said. "You're not that ugly. Well not on the outside anyway."

Just as Paulo started to form a reply, Charles sat upright. "Don't believe everything you read, Paulo," he said quickly. "You know what the papers are like."

"A man of mystery these days?" Paulo asked. "Who would have thought it?"

"Something like that," Charles said with a sickly-sweet smile he didn't mean. "What about you, Luis? You're very quiet today."

Luis had been staring out of the window for most of the flight, not engaging with anyone, including Paulo. Everyone deserved a bit of space, but it did leave his pet stuck for something to do, and annoying Charles and Will seemed to be the only option left to Paulo.

"I'm just focused," Luis muttered

Charles wasn't buying that. They focused when they were

in the cockpit, not in the plane cabin. Luis' face looked as though he had the weight of the world on his shoulders. "You seem to be focused ever since we saw Jeannie last night," he said, knowing he was pushing him.

"Ah yes," Paulo said. "How was the film? Did you boys play nice for Meera?"

Will narrowed his eyes but Charles kicked him under the table. "It was wonderful, thank you. Luis, you should have stayed for the film. It's really good."

"You didn't watch the film?" Will asked.

"He had to focus," Charles replied with a knowing smirk.

The seatbelt signs came to Luis' rescue and the plane made its landing at a private airfield on the outskirts of Monaco.

Charles stared across at Luis. He found his heart going out to him. They had ganged up on him and it wasn't fair.

Will caught his eye and shook his head. Charles responded with a scowl. Why did his brother have to know him so well?

"Fuck it," Charles screamed, throwing his helmet across the room. It ricocheted off the wall and clattered to the floor.

It was qualifier day, where each driver hit the track and lap times denoted their starting position. It hadn't gone well, and he would be in fifth position. It just showed that a driver was only as good as his last race in this game.

To add insult to injury, Luis had achieved pole position, which meant he would be at the front of the pack. The tables had turned. Charles was pleased for him, of course. But Meera and the rest of the world would be watching Charles this race. They would want to know if Bahrain was form or simply a fluke.

Will came into the room after him. He stared at the helmet with chipped paint on the top—Charles had flung it a little more forcefully than he'd intended. "If you wreck that, Meera will charge you," he said.

"I couldn't give a fuck," Charles raged. "I'll buy twenty of them if I like. Fucking fifth?"

"You're being very dramatic," Will replied. "You can make it up."

He would have an uphill struggle. With Jackson Trench and Luis Salvatore defending their positions like tigers, he wouldn't have much chance of getting past them. He had done it before.

His phone rang. Charles clicked Answer. "Meera," he said, pulling a face to Will.

"Fifth isn't great but it isn't the end of the world," she said. "I hope you're not letting it fuck you up. I need you on your A game tomorrow."

Hello to you too. "Is that why you rang me?" he asked. "Very touching." If he wanted the soft-soap approach, it was highly unlikely Meera would be providing it. Nor Barnaby who had totally blanked him and dashed straight to Luis with his congratulations.

Charles did not like being at the bottom of the pile.

"I rang you to say you protect Luis' position," Meera continued. "The best you can hope for is second. Do you understand me?"

Frowning, he tried to process what she asked of him. He understood the team came above everything. Surely she didn't expect him to not give a shit about winning. They had signed the wrong driver for that one. He had no other highs left than racing across that finish line first. "If I see a chance, I'm going for it," he replied, more sulkily than he'd intended.

She sighed as though she were speaking to a five-year-old. "No, Charles. You won't. We move as a team in South Tel. I don't want to have to explain that to you again. Do you understand me?"

Her strategy was flawless, and he had never raced like that

before. Doubt gnawed at him that, in the heat of the moment, he wouldn't be able to follow through on it. He craved the validation of the number one podium. Now his taste for it had been renewed, it was more addictive than the booze. "Yes, of course," he said gruffly.

"I hope so," she continued. "I'll speak to you tomorrow. Listen to Barnaby and support Luis. Those are my final words."

The call terminated before he had a chance to respond. He tried to view himself through her eyes. She had taken a gamble signing him when most other teams wouldn't even give him the time of day. Perhaps he had started well but they had the whole year to get through. She needed more points than that before she allowed Charles into her inner circle. A place where Luis seemed very comfortable.

He'd always been a lone wolf on the track. Teammates had come and gone. The truth be told, he couldn't even name all of them. Charles had simply focused on that chequered flag at the end.

He hung around the track for a while, chatting to the pit crew. They were a decent bunch and had welcomed him with open arms. That had to be something. He liked the banter and a few of them consoled him.

He loved Monaco, such a vibrant and beautiful place packed to the rafters with the rich and powerful. Most race drivers found this to be one of the most important races in the calendar. Monaco had more history and glamour than all the other circuits rolled into one.

His accountant had told him many times to relocate here. It would be great from a tax point of view. However, Charles was a London boy through and through. He felt a duty to contribute to his country, unlike many of his contemporaries.

The spring sunshine came as a welcome relief. Bahrain had been far too hot to do anything in, so he decided to walk to the hotel. There were tons of autograph hunters at the gates. In the past, he would have bypassed them in favour of having a sneaky drink in his room. He had never drunk when driving but the ever-present lure of the vodka bottle would grip him in the safety of his suite.

"Great to have you back, Charles," one eager young man shouted as he walked through the gates.

"Thank you," he replied reaching for an outstretched bit of paper to sign.

"I've never had yours before," the man said with a grin. "You never bother."

Guilt ran over him. Had he really taken his position for granted?

He spent about fifteen minutes chatting to fans and signing everything from programmes to magazines and one woman's leg. His father had warned him that fame wasn't a real thing and he totally understood that. However, today, the attention gave him the boost he needed.

As he broke away, an older man waited slightly apart from the rest of the crowd. He nodded kindly at Charles. "I think you're an inspiration," the man said.

"Me?" Charles asked, in shock. "Really?"

The man nodded. "Keep fighting it."

He found himself welling up with tears. The press had given him a hard time over the years with his heart-breaking, carousing antics. To be known as the bad boy of Formula One had suited him. It hadn't occurred to him that people had been cheering him on. Of course, he got many fan letters. Will generally dealt with all that. To see the support for himself made him humble yet determined.

"Thank you," he said, shaking the man's hand. "Thank you, so much." With a spring in his step, he walked towards the hotel. About halfway along the pavement, his stomach dropped when he saw Paulo. It was too late. the grinning Brazilian had already seen him.

Steeling himself for yet another catty observation, he put on his best fake smile. "Paulo," he said. "How nice to see you."

"Walking to the hotel?" Paulo replied. "Be careful, Charles. People will realise you're only human after all."

Every word this man said came loaded with venom. After the day he'd had, Charles had no desire to trade insults with him. "Don't tell anyone, will you?" he replied. "I would hate to ruin my image."

Charles never stopped walking. To his annoyance, Paulo fell into step with him. Luis was staying at the same hotel so Paulo would be unshakeable until he got safely inside his room.

"Bad luck today," Paulo said with fake concern. "After Bahrain, I suppose you expected to get pole again."

A couple of the pit crew were walking towards them. "Hi, guys," Charles said, high-fiving one, glad of the interruption. "I never expect anything, Paulo. You know how this world works."

"I suppose you're right," Paulo replied. "Luis won here last year. Did you know that?"

"Of course I knew that."

"I wasn't sure if they let you have televisions in rehab."

"Is that supposed to upset me?" Charles asked. "I'm not proud I had to go. I am proud that I am in recovery. Does that make it clear enough for you?"

Paulo patted his arm. "And so you should be."

The touch of the slimy little toad made Charles want to recoil. Strangely he found himself wondering again if he and Luis had ever ended up in bed. He wouldn't put anything past Paulo but surely Luis had better taste than that. "Thanks. Your approval means the world," he said, drily.

"Luis told me he had a great time at lunch the other day," Paulo continued.

Had Luis given his secret away? He did not seem the type to gossip, especially about something so deeply personal.

"Oh, yes?" he asked. Thankfully the hotel was in sight. This odious little creep had begun to make him feel sick.

"Bit strange to take him to a movie though," Paulo mused. "Especially an old man's one."

His tolerance wore thin now. "Is there something you needed, Paulo?"

"Not at all," Paulo replied as fake as possible. Charles wanted to slap him. "I just thought I'd make sure you got to the hotel safely. You really shouldn't wander around on a race weekend. Even if you have to get out your aggression. There's a gym for that."

Charles walked through the hotel's doors. "No aggression here, Paulo. I think you're misreading things again. A fifth-place start is decent."

Once more, Paulo patted his arm. "I'm sure it is. Not every weekend can be a podium finish."

He walked through the door and stalked across the reception. Charles watched him go.

You want a podium finish? I'll show you one.

CHAPTER EIGHT

"Stay back, Charles," his controller barked down the headset. "You know the script. Defend second place."

Luis was the only one ahead of him now. Charles had easily got to third position. Jackson Trench hadn't given him an inch, but just as they'd gone into the final lap, Charles had managed to get past him. Now both South Tel drivers held the top two spots. They had the podium in their sights. Charles should block Trench and give Luis a free run to the chequered flag.

Paulo's words kept echoing in his mind. That little shit had ruined his victory in Bahrain, and he would love to goad Charles that he hadn't won here. He sped dangerously close to Luis as they took a hairpin bend.

"What are you doing, Charles?" the controller said, traces of panic in his voice.

Trying to clear his mind, Charles focused on the prize. Meera couldn't argue which one of them won the race and which came second. He wanted to show the world that Charles Worthington had regained his crown, and pole position twice in a row would silence everyone.

As Meera flashed into his mind, he remembered she knew

about him. It could only have come from Luis. Determination flooded through his system.

I'll show them all that I'm a serious contender.

He slammed his right foot on the accelerator. Charles would get as much out of this baby as possible. The data readout told him it was a bad idea, but with one lap to go, where was the risk? He would show them all what Charles Worthington was made of.

"Charles. For fuck's sake," Barnaby's stern voice filled his ears. He must have ripped the headset from poor Bob, the controller.

He focused himself on the prize as they approached the final part of the track. He would zoom up behind Luis then at the last minute, take him. Charles had done this manoeuvre a hundred times. In fact, it was his speciality. Letting the car get as close as he dared, he could make out the back of Luis' head.

"Abort, Charles," Barnaby raged.

"Negative," he replied.

They took the last bend of the track at top speed and Charles readied himself to pull out on the home stretch. Luis braked harder than he'd anticipated, and Charles clipped his rear tyre.

Suddenly Charles didn't know which way was up and which was down as his car spun violently. He gripped the steering wheel hard and held his breath as the powerful machine slammed into the side of the track, knocking the air out of his lungs.

Dazed for a second, Charles managed to focus. Smoke poured out of the front of his car. He had to get out and fast. Freeing himself from the safety constraints, he managed to crawl out of the cockpit. To his horror, he saw Luis' car also smashed up at the side of the track.

What had he done?

Officials and crew were sprinting towards them. Luis hadn't

moved yet. Terror washed over Charles. On unsteady legs, he dashed over to Luis.

"Are you okay?" he shouted through his helmet.

Luis' car didn't seem to be on fire. Not wanting to chance it, Charles clawed at his body. The touch of another human being must have brought Luis round and between them, they managed to get him out and onto the track.

By now the fire crews were putting the flames out on Charles' car. He and Luis moved away to safety.

"Do you feel okay?" a paramedic asked him.

Charles felt like the biggest twat in Europe. It was amazing that drivers walked away from such crashes these days. The ramifications when he got to the pit would have a much deeper impact. He took his helmet off at the same time as Luis. The pure venom on Luis' face made Charles' stomach contract.

"I'm so sorry," he said. It sounded impotent and pathetic, but he had no other words.

Luis threw his helmet against the wall and just stared at Charles. "I had it," Luis snarled. "I fucking had it, you motherfucker."

To his horror, Luis marched towards him. The rage radiating from him made Charles take a step back. He lost his footing on a piece of tyre and fell backwards, hitting the ground with a jolt. Then Luis was on him.

The first blow smashed into Charles face. He felt a sickening crack. He got his hands over his face before the second blow came in. He grabbed Luis and they struggled. Luis rained punches into his body. The anger attached to every one of them terrified Charles. He had never been a fighter and only defended himself.

"You fucking bastard," Luis spat.

Thankfully, a crew member dragged Luis off Charles and he struggled to regain his composure. Getting to his feet, he started the long walk to the pit. Today would not be a good day.

Charles had flatly refused to do any press after the race. It would make him even less popular in Barnaby's eyes but tough luck. He had no desire to spend hours telling people what a dickhead he was. Instead, he'd sat in his little room. He'd even forbidden Will from visiting. Charles desperately craved a drink. He didn't dare leave the confines of the pit and into temptation.

Also, he did not want to run into Luis again. Charles had to stabilise himself, even if people thought him a coward. Closing his eyes, he concentrated entirely on his breathing. This had been a stupid fucking setback. He couldn't use it as an excuse to drink though.

Slowly he began to separate the shit from that day with his need for booze. He would deal with the ramifications of his actions far better sober. Gradually, the need began to shrink. Charles continued to breathe and work on it. Two hours later, he emerged from his room. Will sat on a chair outside.

"Ready?" he asked.

Charles nodded and allowed him to lead him out to the waiting vehicle. A few of the crew who had lingered around didn't meet his gaze.

"What a dick," Will said, when they reached the safety of the SUV.

There would be no walking and lapping up the crowd's adoration today. A few people banged on the car as they drove through. They took Formula One very seriously in Monaco.

"Don't you start," Charles grumbled. "What was I fucking thinking?" He put his head in his hands, the urge to burst into tears a very real threat.

"You made a bad call," Will soothed. "It's not the first time and it probably won't be the last."

Charles frowned. "Is that the best you can do?"

Shrugging, Will stared out of the window. "I thought I did very well, actually."

They drove the rest of the way in silence. When he'd made a fuck-up, and there had been plenty of those over the years, Charles retreated into his head. Will knew this and gave him the space he needed.

When they arrived at the hotel, photographers swarmed everywhere. Charles groaned. He'd expected it. Even so, dealing with it took a lot of inner strength.

Then he saw her standing on the steps of the hotel, tapping her foot with a face like thunder. Hilary Milligan might only be five foot tall, but she struck fear into the hearts of anyone who came into contact with her. She had built a formidable reputation on the celebrity circuit, earning the nickname the Piranha PR. He had suffered her wrath countless times. She also protected him fiercely.

Seeing his car, she started barking orders at the terrified doormen, who snapped to attention. In no time, she cleared a way for him to dash through the clicking shutters and into the hotel reception. "You," she said to him. "That door over there."

He made his way over to where her taloned finger pointed. Will made to join him but Hilary got in his way.

"Just my client for now," she said. "I think you can find somewhere ridiculously expensive for you and I to have dinner. We need to discuss things."

Shrugging, Will gave him a wink. A small gesture gratefully received. It meant he had his back. Sometimes Charles didn't know how he would cope without him.

The meeting room was small but thankfully windowless. Still in his racing suit, Charles sat down at the table. He leapt sky high when Hilary came in and slammed the door shut behind her.

"What the fuck?" she said, simply.

"When did you get here?" he replied.

"Don't answer a question with a question," she continued. "What were you thinking?"

Charles put his head in his hands. "I don't fucking know, do I? I wanted it so badly I couldn't see anything else."

Hilary paced around the room like a caged animal. "That's pretty fucking obvious," she said. "This feud shit is bad for business, Charles. Meera gave me so much shit down the phone. She wanted to send bloody Varma to sort this out, but I told her, you're my client and I know how you tick. That was a fucking lie because I don't even think you know that. You dozy twat."

"You got here pretty bloody quick. I've only been off the track two hours."

Hilary sat, rubbing her temples. "Money can make anything happen. What is going on?"

The tears welled. Charles hated crying in front of people. "It all feels different, Hil," he said, wiping his eyes with the back of his hand. "I don't know who I am anymore."

"Have you spoken to Luis?" she asked. To his relief she had adopted a slightly kinder tone. He might get away with a light savaging instead of her going for his jugular.

"I wanted to. He went straight to the press conference," Charles lied. "Barnaby thought it best that I keep a low profile."

Even if he had spoken to Luis, what would he say?

"I agree," Hilary said. "In fact, I think you should go to your room now and leave it to me. I'll do as much damage limitation as I can. You're going to have to get a bloody good excuse together though. We'll give Terry at *The Racer* an exclusive and hopefully that will be that. Let's face it, Charles Worthington acting like a knob again isn't exactly headline material."

He had hoped the press would never run another one of those stories. He'd lasted two races into his new season. "Fine," he sighed, getting up. "I could do with some space anyway."

Hilary narrowed her eyes. "I'll get the lowdown from your brother about what's been going on," she said. "But mark my words, I don't want to have to come to every bloody race. Too much testosterone for me."

"I promise, you won't have to." He went to make his way out of the room.

"And don't think you're off the hook about attending a Nihal fucking Varma event either," Hilary said. "Not by a long chalk."

Without bothering to reply, he sloped out of the room. The photographers spotted him through the glass doors and the machine-gun-like cameras opened fire. A lot of people were milling around the reception area. All eyes were on him, yet he didn't care. Let them criticise. When had they ever won a fucking Grand Prix?

He rode the lift in silence, hardly able to look at his reflection in the mirrors. They would be flying home in the morning and no doubt Luis would be on the flight. With Paulo who would be loving every minute of this. Of that, Charles had no doubt and it annoyed him even more.

The suite had a decent-sized lounge with small kitchen off to the side, and the view over the marina was exemplary. Tonight, Charles had no desire to watch obscenely expensive boats. In the blue and white bedroom, he stripped off. He desperately needed a shower to wash the day's woes away.

Then he stopped. On the bedside table sat a bottle of vodka.

Where the fuck has that come from?

On all of Charles' reservations were strict instructions that all rooms be cleansed of alcohol. Mini bars were stripped and even room service menus were reprinted. He walked over to the bottle and ran his finger down it. The temptation to take a tiny swig, just to take the edge off, gripped him.

No one would have to know.

Then he caught sight of himself in the huge mirror behind the bed. His naked reflection stopped him in his tracks. He was leaner and healthier than he had been in years. Storming into the bathroom, he powered up the huge monsoon shower and stood under the jets. All the while, the vodka bottle seemed to be calling to him.

Do I have the strength to pour it down this drain?

When he'd got home after rehab, he had made a big deal of pouring every bottle in the house away. Will had thought it a terrible waste. Well, he would. Charles had never experienced a feeling of power like that before. Even driving a top-of-the-range race car paled into comparison of taking control of his own life. No matter who had left that bottle in his room, he vowed they would not ruin things for him.

Wrapping one of the impossibly fluffy towels around him, he marched into the bedroom and grabbed the offending item. Before he had the chance to evict it from his life, there came a hammering on the door. South Tel had security on the corridors, so they had to be authorised. He hoped to God it wasn't Meera. He didn't fancy a dressing down from her at that moment.

He slammed the vodka bottle on the dining table and yanked open the door.

There stood a furious Luis.

CHAPTER NINE

To say Charles was underdressed was putting it mildly. Luis looked incredible in blue pleated shorts and a white polo shirt. He had a South Tel baseball cap on. It did nothing to shield Charles from the abject rage on Luis' face.

"You'd better come in," Charles said, miserably.

Luis barged past him and into the suite.

"Whatever you have to say, I'll take it," Charles continued, letting the door shut behind him. "But please don't hit me again."

"Worried about your promotional duties?" Luis sneered.

"No, it fucking hurts," Charles replied. He still had a dull ache in his jaw. Luis packed a punch. He sat on the white leather sofa and gestured for Luis to take the opposite one. He should probably go and get changed. In a fit of optimism, he hoped Luis would run out of steam quickly and leave him to his night.

"Why are you trying to ruin my season?" Luis asked.

Once again, Charles thought him slightly melodramatic. "I made a bad call," Charles replied. "I got wound up before the race and I let it rule my head. I'm a total twat and I sincerely apologise."

He had never liked the taste of humble pie. It was even more bitter with Luis. The more time he spent with him, the more he wanted to impress him. He would have to work very hard to regain the small amount of ground they had made over recent weeks.

Luis stood and walked over to the window. "I want to believe you, but it feels like you're out to prove a point. I can understand that. Not at my expense though, Charles. It's unfair."

"I know what it feels like to have it taken from you like that," Charles said. "Trench did that to me in Saudi a couple of years ago. I would never do it to you purposefully. Please believe that."

Luis sighed. He had the weight of the world on his shoulders and Charles had put it there. The guilt was immense. "I think there is more to this," Luis said. "We need to get this out or we'll both lose this season. I don't think you can afford that, and I bloody know I can't."

Charles got up and joined him at the window. Below them, wealthy people in designer labels packed the marina. Monaco had a well-earned reputation as a party town and Grand Prix night was one of the biggest nights in the calendar. He'd had plenty of good times there. It all seemed a million miles away as he stood next to Luis.

"Can I ask you something?" he said.

Luis stared at him, intrigued. "You want a favour from me?"

"Not a favour," Charles replied. "But the truth. Did you tell Meera about my sexuality?"

Taking a step back, Luis looked as though he'd been slapped. "Of course not. I told you I wouldn't tell anyone, and I meant it. Why?"

"She knows."

Frowning, Luis seemed lost in thought. "Everyone knows you like both," he said. "Perhaps she just made an assumption."

"I don't think so," Charles replied. "It's not your problem. I'm not trying to make excuses. With that and Paulo..."

Luis stared hard at him. "What about Paulo?"

"Nothing," Charles replied, hastily. "He tried to get under my skin yesterday. I need to learn to handle it."

They were standing close together. Charles desperately wanted to reach out and run his finger down Luis' smooth cheek. He wondered how soft the skin would be to the touch.

"Paulo has a terrible mouth on him," Luis said. "I'll tell him to lay off."

"I don't deserve it."

"No, you don't."

They maintained eye contact yet neither spoke. Charles heard his heart pumping in his chest. Luis broke the stare first and glanced around the room. His gaze stopped at the dining table with the bottle of vodka standing proudly to attention. "What is that?" he asked.

Once again, Charles felt terrible that this sweet man had come to his room with the express intention of laying into him and now he was full of concern. "Not what it looks like," he replied. "When I got here, it had been left on my bedside table. I was about to pour it away when you came smashing through the door like a caveman."

Luis chuckled. "It should really be too soon for jokes, you know."

"Jokes at inappropriate times are one of my specialities."

The smile drained from Luis' face. "Were you tempted?"

Charles sighed. "Like you wouldn't believe."

Luis went over to the table and picked up the bottle.

"See," Charles said. "The seal isn't broken."

"The hotel should be ashamed of themselves for letting this in your room," Luis said, angrily.

Charles grabbed the bottle and walked through into the butler's kitchen. With every last morsel of resolve, he opened the vodka and poured it down the sink. Once again, that intoxicating feeling of control flooded through his system. He had told himself he would fight temptation and now, with Luis watching him, he had beaten it again.

"There," he said, walking over to the window. "Now finish having a go and leave me be."

Joining him at the window, Luis regarded Charles carefully. Once more, Charles luxuriated in those steely blue eyes being trained on him. Their effect knocked him off balance every time.

"Now I want to get to the bottom of what is going on," Luis said, slowly. "I have watched you for years and I refuse to believe everything was down to booze. You are usually so in control of things. Nothing stops Charles Worthington."

Charles welled up. "I don't know where my place is anymore," he began. "That man seems like a lifetime ago. Rehab did more than make me face my booze demons. It made me examine everything. No stone left unturned. Every single mistake I've made in life had a dirty great spotlight on it."

Luis took in the opulent suite. "A lot of people would say you'd done okay."

Charles had found that the world didn't accept successful people having problems. Everyone thought he had no right to flounder. That made the pressure to cope even greater. "It feels like..."

Down in the marina, people were flitting around the uber-expensive yachts. They didn't have a care in the world. They probably thought the same about him.

"What? Go on," Luis said, softly.

"It feels like I've been reprogrammed and I don't fit into my life anymore," Charles said, meeting his gaze. "If you must know, you intimidate me."

Luis burst out laughing. "I intimidate you? That's ridiculous. How?"

"Because you're everything I'm not," Charles said, seriously. "You're gorgeous inside and out, you know exactly who you are and where you're going to. You terrify me."

Luis looked confused. "You are not who I expected you to be either," he said, softly.

"I don't want to be him anymore," Charles explained. "I guess for the first time, I'm not even trying to be."

They were inches away from each other and every fibre of Charles' being told him to make that last jump and kiss Luis. He'd made so many bad judgements recently he feared making things worse.

"And you expect me to throw away my chances of winning races and help you do this?" Luis murmured.

"Of course not," Charles replied. He heard the nerves in his voice. "I want us to be unstoppable." He took the tiniest of steps forward. Luis didn't repel him, which had to be a good thing.

"On the track?" Luis whispered.

"Everywhere."

Luis leaned forward and kissed him. The waves of relief cascaded over Charles' body like a tsunami. It appeared that Luis felt the same as he ran his hand around Charles' waist. It sent tingles throughout Charles' body, his skin becoming goose-flesh at Luis' touch.

His cock had fired into life quicker than Ferrari's new super-car. The towel had no chance of hiding this. Luis drew him closer, so Charles' erection pressed against his thigh.

"Well, well," Luis said as they broke the kiss. "Looks like something is unstoppable."

"Want to take this to the bedroom?" Charles said. "I've had enough of paparazzi for one day and fuck knows who's got their lens on us right now."

Luis bit his lip. "Is this really a good idea? We could be making a huge fucking error. After all, I came here to kick the shit out of you again."

He might as well have thrown Charles straight into an ice bath. "I think this will fix things," Charles said. "I mean it. At least from my side. If you have reservations, that's cool." He tried to sound as nonchalant as possible. In reality, his legs were shaking.

Luis grinned. "Fucking hell. Charles Worthington has changed. Lead the way."

Most of his sex life had been played out either drunk or recently with the deal being done on a faceless app before they even arrived on his doorstep. He found himself in a whole different arena. Nerves flew round his system like cars on a circuit.

He *was* Charles Worthington, and that reputation hadn't only been vodka fuelled. Reaching down, he flicked the towel around his waist and let it fall to the floor. The gasp that came from Luis made him smile. He might be older, but he was still in pretty good shape.

"Wow," Luis said. He darted forward and grabbed Charles by the waist, pressing his fully clothed body against Charles' naked back. Luis kissed him on the side of the neck and wrapped his hands around his chest. The smell of Luis sent Charles into overdrive. A musky scent that screamed sex.

Through his jeans, Charles felt Luis' solid cock. He pushed back, letting his arse grind against him. Wriggling free of Luis' grasp, he crawled onto the huge bed that he'd pictured himself having a sleepless night in. Perhaps he still would have but for far more exciting reasons than replaying the race over and over in his mind.

"Get them off," Charles murmured. Settling against the huge pillows, he lazily stroked his cock while he watched Luis pulling his clothes off. "Slowly. Let me enjoy it."

Luis threw his T-shirt at him. "Fuck that."

By the time Charles whipped the T-shirt away, Luis was butt naked and crawling on the bed.

"I can see you don't do orders," Charles observed.

Luis climbed on top of him and the sensation of their skin on skin made Charles' cock ache all the more. Staring into his eyes, Luis smirked. "I've never been good at orders," he whispered.

They kissed. Charles ran his fingers over Luis' skin. It was so toned yet soft. As he lightly traced over his arse cheek, the anticipation at exploring this body became almost too much. He had slept with more women and men than he wanted to admit to, but something about this with Luis was different. They had a closeness that Charles had never experienced before.

Luis kissed him again, harder and hungrier. Charles' heartrate sped up as they rolled around the bed. Now Charles was on top of Luis. He wanted to give him as much pleasure as possible. Pulling away from his mouth, he kissed Luis' neck, making him moan with pleasure. Charles loved finding those spots that sent people into the next stratosphere. Glancing at Luis, he caught his eye and winked.

"Corny," Luis murmured.

Charles moved off him and kneeled at his side. He took the opportunity to examine Luis' body. He found it impossible to leave Luis' hairless tan skin alone. Running his hands over him, he let his fingers travel down to Luis' hard cock. When he grasped hold, Luis cried out.

"Oh God, that feels good."

Charles gently stroked him, taking pleasure in the precum that glistened on the head. Leaning down, he rolled his tongue over it and sucked the tip. The salty taste exploding on his tongue made him want more. Unable to wait any longer, he took Luis fully in his mouth.

Once again, Luis cried out, grasping the sheets as Charles sucked him hard. He had wanted to know what it would feel like for so long and the reality didn't disappoint. All the stresses of the day were disappearing as Charles and Luis found a new way to connect. He would never have believed he would end the day like this.

Luis gently held his head as he slid up and down the shaft. Fuck Luis tasted good.

"Oh fuck," he whispered. "Stop or I'll come."

Charles moved away and took Luis' hand. He led it to his own cock. "I need to come," Charles replied. "Now."

Sharing his urgency, Luis got up and pushed him down against the pillow. He positioned himself between his legs and licked the length of Charles' hard dick. The sensation drove Charles crazy.

"Don't tease me," he begged. He wanted to take it so slowly, but the urge overpowered him. He needed the release that only an orgasm could bring.

At last, Luis wrapped his lips around Charles' solid cock and started to suck. He wouldn't last long and gave himself up to the incredible sensation. He watched Luis expertly controlling him and couldn't believe how lucky he was. Luis had to be one of the best-looking men he'd ever met, and he'd met a few. Beyond his physical appearance, they had something between them that transcended that. It scared Charles a little.

With his free hand, Luis pulled at his own cock. The sight was too much for Charles and he arched his back. "I'm going to come," he gasped.

This made Luis suck all the harder until Charles' orgasm exploded in his mouth. His whole body surrendered to pleasure for that wonderful split second. Crying out, he thrashed against the pillow.

When he stilled, Luis straddled his now spent cock. To feel Luis' unexplored hole rubbing against him made Charles vow there would be no sleep that night. Luis massaged himself. Charles reached forward and cupped his balls. "Come for me," he whispered.

Luis didn't need much more persuading and thrust his head

back. He let out a yell as he came, his muscles contracting with pleasure. Charles ran his hands over Luis' hard body. He couldn't resist that soft yet toned skin he'd only just begun to explore fully. As the last judder made its way through Luis' system, he opened his eyes and met Charles' gaze. "Well, that was short and sweet," he panted.

"You'll have to stay the night then," Charles replied, holding his arm out.

Luis snuggled into him. "Now that sounds like a plan."

CHAPTER TEN

The moonlight shone through the gaps in the curtains, a slight breeze making it dance on the white coffee table in the lounge. Charles lay on the sofa with Luis in his arms. Far below, late party animals were hollering to each other.

"If the press saw us now," Luis said, kissing Charles forearm.

"That would make a story," Charles replied, nuzzling the top of his head.

The bed lay in a mess where they'd spent hours finding each other. Charles was usually the type to come and go. Tonight he never wanted to stop holding Luis in his arms. The relief that he hadn't completely fucked it up on the track still fresh in his mind. "I never thought I'd get a blow job and a punch from you in the same day," he continued.

Luis slapped his arm. "You were still an arsehole," he replied. "No matter what."

"I know," Charles replied. "I will be better. I promise."

The silence that followed was an easy one. For the first time since way before rehab, Charles had a sense of peace that came as a welcome relief. He hoped he wasn't reading too much into this. He stood to get hurt otherwise.

"It's hard," Luis said. "Coming out as gay. Especially in our game."

"You managed it pretty well."

Luis sighed and stroked Charles' fingers, letting his own clasp them.

"You have no idea what it was like behind the scenes," Luis continued. "My agent and my family told me to keep quiet, but I told them I had to be myself. Why should I hide?"

Charles remembered the newspaper headlines. Luis had been in his first season and the rest of the drivers thought he had committed career suicide. He might carry on racing, but the sponsorships would surely dry up.

The reality had been anything but. Luis was currently the face of a fashion line, an aftershave, a luxury car brand, and an airline. It appeared the world had underestimated the power of the pink pound. Luis had ploughed most of the money into the Luis Salvatore Foundation which fought poverty in his native Brazil as well as funding LGBTQ projects all over the world.

"Look at what you achieved," Charles said. "You're the Mother Theresa of Formula One."

"I did my best for my family," Luis replied, seriously. "They sacrificed so much for me to have this life, it's only right that I pay them back. I'm proud that I've lifted fifty of them out of poverty. Aunts, uncles, cousins, the lot."

Charles squeezed him tightly. His family had never wanted for money. "Fifty?" he asked. "That's incredible. Plus, your foundation. I don't know how you find the time to race."

"Racing is the only thing I have to focus on. Paulo works with my people to make sure the money gets spent properly."

Charles thought about his latest meeting with his accountant. Even though he'd been out of the game for a year, his income hadn't suffered all that much. He had more in the bank than he would ever spend. The realisation that he had never really used his position for anything good dawned on him.

"I've only ever gone to charity things because it's a good party," he admitted. "I want you to help me to be a better person."

Luis shifted to the end of the sofa, so they were staring at each other. "Are you saying this isn't a one-off?"

The big question.

"Well, you haven't let me fuck you yet," Charles replied. How he would love to fuck that solid arse.

"I'm being serious, Charles," Luis said. "A night of sex is one thing."

Fear gripped Charles as the realisation that he'd completely misread this dawned on him. "Oh...shit, sorry," he said, sitting up. "Have I just made a fool of myself?"

Luis reached across and took his hand. "Not at all. I'm just surprised. Charles Worthington wanting more. I thought you were all about the bedpost notches."

Charles took hold of his hand. Luis' touch made his fears evaporate. Sylvia, his counsellor, had told him that he had to be honest. Carrying around the burden of the "public" Charles Worthington had been the main reason he had turned to the bottle in the first place. Charles had always been confident, whether at school or racing, but the constant need to be on duty had taken its toll. "I'd like to see what the new Charles is like."

"So would I," Luis replied.

They kissed. It felt like a deal had been made although Charles had no idea what his side of the bargain was.

"As for fucking," Luis said, "that will come in time. If you behave yourself."

Charles wasn't used to being refused, especially in the bedroom. He found he quite liked it. "Consider it done," he replied.

"I think we should probably keep it to ourselves for the time being," Luis said, settling against the cushions.

Once again, Charles drank in his perfect body. The six-pack

that Charles had planted kisses on, the solid thighs he'd gripped, and the cock he'd sucked. "You mean best not let Paulo know," he muttered.

Luis sighed. "I know you don't like him. He's very important to me though. I want you to respect that."

Charles frowned. "What gives with you two?"

Absentmindedly stroking Charles' calf, Luis took a breath. "We go back almost to birth. His mum and my mum are best friends. We arrived about two weeks apart. He's older. Something I like to remind him."

Paulo wouldn't like that. Mind you, he'd created a whole career in following Luis. He was hardly in a position to complain. "So why the attitude to me?" Charles asked.

"He's protective," Luis answered. "You're a player, Charles. It's common knowledge. He said we'd end up in bed."

Paulo was astute if nothing else. Charles hated being predictable. He would make an exception if it meant getting more time with Luis' incredible body. "Sounds like he's jealous, to me," Charles said sniffily. "I bet—"

He stopped himself. They might have found a new level of understanding, but the shaky ground they had built it on didn't need upsetting.

"You bet what?"

"Nothing."

"Go on, I hate that."

"Okay, I bet he left that vodka in there."

Luis flushed. "He wouldn't do that."

"He fucking would."

Getting up off the sofa, Luis walked over to the window. It would be dawn soon and the real world would come knocking. "He's my friend, Charles. I won't hear shit about him."

Charles got up and walked behind Luis. He clasped his arms around him. "I'm sorry," he said. "Forgive me?"

Luis shrugged. "I think you should probably earn that forgiveness."

Wordlessly, Charles sank to his knees, his face inches from that incredible cock which had already started to swell. The power that gave him made Charles higher than any drug or drink. Licking at it, he stared up at Luis. Framed in the moon's glow, he gave off the aura of a beautiful painting.

Oh Jesus, Worthington. This is trouble.

He took Luis in his mouth, the soft flesh of his part erection making Charles so horny. As he sucked, Luis hardened. This sent triggers directly to Charles' cock that sprang to attention. Charles ran his mouth up and down the now solid length of Luis' cock. The taste of him once again made Charles moan.

With his free hands, he took hold of Luis' arse cheeks. Gripping hard, he controlled Luis fucking his mouth. Luis ran his hands through Charles' curls.

"Oh, God. Charles," Luis stammered. "I'm going to come." Thrusting into Charles' mouth, Luis tightened his grip on his head. Charles wanted to pleasure him so badly, his own cock was aching. The salty taste of Luis made his tastebuds dance. He steadied himself to let Luis fuck his mouth harder. Charles took hold of Luis' thighs, driving him in and out of his mouth.

Come on, baby, let me taste you.

He didn't have to wait long until Luis cried out once more. Suddenly, Charles' mouth was filled with the bittersweet cum he had been craving. He didn't move until every last drop had been spilt. Then he licked Luis' dick clean. He didn't want to waste any of it. It was part of Luis and it was hot that it was inside him now.

Sitting back, he watched a trembling Luis sink onto the sofa.

"Fuck, that was amazing," Luis panted.

Charles crawled next to him. He licked the sweat sheening on Luis' chest. Every part of this man tasted so good. Happily, he settled into Luis' arms and they dozed for a while, the steady thrum of Luis' heart sending Charles to sleep.

About an hour into it and someone decided to set off a ton of fireworks. They illuminated the room in pinks and reds and blues.

"What time is it?" Luis asked, rubbing his eyes.

"Don't ask that," Charles replied. "You'll burst our bubble."

Luis kissed him. "Bubbles are made to be burst. Don't worry, I'll blow you a new one."

"Fine." Charles sighed. "It's ten o'clock. It's not even late." He nuzzled into Luis' neck. This man did something to him that scared and excited him all at once.

"We need to be at the plane early. I don't fancy us being clocked leaving the same suite," Luis said.

Suddenly there was a loud knock at the door.

"Fuck." Charles, jumped out of his skin. "'It's ten o'clock. Who the fuck is that?"

"I'll stay in the bedroom. Get rid of them," Luis replied.

Luis ran into the next room and threw a bathrobe out. For the second time that night, someone clearly wanted to hammer the door in.

Is there no fucking peace?

"All right," Charles shouted. When he opened it, the glaring face of Barnaby greeted him.

"Good evening," he said.

"Barnaby," Charles began. "If you've..."

But the Team Principal wasn't for being put off. He marched into the suite.

"Come in then," Charles said, closing the door behind them.

Barnaby stared around the suite as though he were scanning for something. "I didn't come and see you earlier. Your guard dog, Ms Milligan, suggested I leave you be for the evening although why I'm taking orders from a PR woman is beyond me. So here I am."

Still tasting Luis on his tongue, Charles wondered what Barnaby would have thought if he'd seen what they were doing only minutes before. That really would get his knickers in a twist. Barnaby sat on the couch. Charles had a flashback to holding Luis in his arms on that exact spot only minutes before. He sat on the opposite sofa.

"Barnaby," Charles said. "I have spoken to Luis and when we get home, I will make a speech to the team. I let things get the better of me and I made the biggest fuckup of my career."

"Meera is ready to kill you," Barnaby replied. "You should probably make a speech to her before the team."

Meera. He dreaded facing her.

"I will prove to you that I can do this," Charles said.

"You're lucky you have Bahrain to fall back on," Barnaby replied. "You'd be fucked without that."

Thankfully it was early in the season and Charles had plenty of chances to show South Tel that things were different now. He wished he could tell them why, but Luis had made it clear that wasn't an option. "I let things get on top of me," he said, quietly. "I knew it would be difficult, returning to the circuits. I forgot the extra pressures."

Barnaby raised an eyebrow. "Extra pressures?"

Charles sat forward. He didn't want Luis to overhear this. "Someone planted a bottle of vodka in my room tonight," he explained. "I have a fair idea who."

"And? Did you drink it?"

How dare he question him like this? Did he look like he'd been on a bender? Then he realised that he probably did come across like he'd been put through a bush backwards. They had had quite the evening. Hopefully Barnaby would put that down to worrying. "Of course I didn't. I threw it in the sink in there. Go and find the empty bottle if you don't believe me."

"And who do you think is setting traps?"

"I've no real clue," Charles said. "I suspect Paulo."

"Have you said anything to him or Luis?"

"Should I?"

"Probably best not to...because I put it there."

Charles reared up as though Barnaby said he was holding a hand grenade. "What the actual fuck?" he exclaimed.

Barnaby just shrugged. His icy-cool demeanour never wavered, no matter what. Charles had no idea what the hell motivated him. He shared the urge to win, but even Charles drew the line at risking someone's recovery and health.

"I wanted to test you," Barnaby replied. "If you're unravelling on our time, I want to know sooner rather than later."

Rage swirled around in Charles' chest. All he wanted to do was smash his fist into Barnaby's cruel face. However, the universe had given him the chance to end this shitty day on a high and he wasn't going to fuck that up. "I trust I passed it," he managed. He tried to match Barnaby's sub-zero tone. The waver in his voice ruined that.

Barnaby stood up and held his hand out. "You did."

"I think you should probably leave now," Charles said. He stood, letting Barnaby's hand hang.

"Fair enough," Barnaby conceded. "Get some sleep."

Giving the suite another once-over, Barnaby walked to the door and wordlessly let himself out. Charles remained stock-still, absolutely stunned. The bedroom door opened, and a naked Luis stood there.

"I suppose you heard all that," Charles said.

Luis nodded.

"What a fucking bastard trick," Charles blurted out. "That's cruel."

He was shaking now. Luis crossed the room and took him in his arms.

"Hey now," Luis said. "He doesn't realise how awful it is. Tell you what though."

"What?"

"This gives you the perfect deflection from a grade-A Meera tongue lashing."

Charles laughed despite himself. He kissed Luis and buried his face in his neck. "You have a weird touch of the Mary Poppins about you, Luis Salvatore," he said.

"Then you'd better get in the bedroom," Luis ordered, "spit spot."

Allowing himself to be dragged into the next room, Charles let the tension leave him. The bubble hadn't burst yet and he wanted to get every last bit of pleasure from it.

CHAPTER ELEVEN

"What's going on with you?" Alexander panted.

Charles stole a look at him. "I don't know what you mean," he replied.

"Stop," Alexander managed.

They ground to a halt. Alexander held on to a tree for support. "Fuck, it's been a while since we did this," he spluttered.

"You're getting out of condition." Charles laughed, clapping him on the shoulder.

Hyde Park was quiet. They were in the lull where the commuters had found their desks, but the tourists hadn't finished their breakfasts yet.

"We've only done one circuit," Alexander complained, "and I'm ready for the knackers yard."

"Poor you," Charles said, getting his breath back. He managed that a whole lot better these days. Back when he had been a regular on the party circuit, his health had been bad. He'd even found himself panting as he climbed the stairs at Harvey Nichols.

Alexander straightened up and gave Charles his best

outraged glare. "You are a cheeky bugger. I'll have you know I'm one of the leading stars on *Celebrity Blogger* soon."

They both caught each other's eye and burst into hysterics.

"It will piss father off if nothing else," Alexander said. "Anyway, that's a diversion tactic. There's only one thing that puts such a pathetic grin on someone's face. You've been getting some."

Charles wondered if he was walking around with a stupid grin. He must be if Alexander had twigged. "I might have been," he replied, mysteriously.

Alexander regarded him carefully. "Well, it agrees with you," he said, taking a swig from his water bottle. "Now let's run back to the Crescent. If you're expected to perform bedroom gymnastics, we'd better get your stamina up."

They jogged through the streets of Knightsbridge. Alexander always insisted they ran past Harrods. He said that seeing all the clothes in the window inspired him to run faster so he could fit into them.

Soon enough though, they made it home.

"I'll have to get Mrs Wimpole onto you," Alexander said as he stood on his steps. "I don't like secrets."

"Don't you dare," Charles replied. "She'll put two and two together and make a hundred."

The lucky thing about Mrs Wimpole was that she hated the press. She might have the goings on of the area under surveillance, but she would never give them away. She had more money than God and thoroughly enjoyed the fact that she remained many steps ahead of the papers when it came to her famous neighbours.

"I'm only teasing," Alexander continued. "Seriously, I know you've been through it so if you need someone to talk to, knock on my door. I have a wonderful array of herbal teas."

Charles appreciated the offer and winked at Alexander. In the house, he found Will in the downstairs lounge.

"Another run?" Will asked. "You two will get papped."

"I don't care," Charles replied, swigging water. "He's a decent guy."

He and Alexander had been neighbours for years. It wasn't until lockdown they had struck up conversation. Then, when it had been allowed, they had taken to jogging together. Charles really enjoyed having a friend not connected to Formula One in any form.

"I'm pleased for the both of you," Will said.

Charles detected a hint of jealousy. Will did like being everything to Charles. He needed to let him have space too. Will took his job as protector of Charles very seriously. Sometimes, though, it could be stifling.

"What time are we on?" Charles replied, ignoring Will's jealous tone.

"You have ten minutes," Will replied "You want coffee?"

Charles nodded.

He dashed up the stairs and threw his sweaty shorts and running top into the laundry bin. His sweaty socks and boxers followed. He viewed himself in the huge floor-to-ceiling mirror that dominated one wall of his dressing room.

Not bad, Worthington.

Forty might be rapidly approaching but he could still turn a head or two. He had never worried about his age before. Now, Luis being younger and far more level-headed than him made Charles uncharacteristically nervous.

"Your brew is ready. This is your five-minute call."

He didn't have time for a shower so instead he put on his South Tel jogging suit. It might earn him a tiny Brownie point with Meera. Something he desperately needed at that moment.

Charles bounded down the stairs lightly, unlike his heavy-footed brother. Will had the laptop set up in the kitchen. Meera's stern face waited for him.

"Ah, Meera," he said. "You're early."

"You're not," she replied. "I haven't got all day. What the fuck?"

Glancing at Will, Charles took a deep breath. "There is nothing I can say but sorry," he began. "I lost my bloody mind out there and all I could see was winning. I forgot about the team, and I promise you, Meera, that will never happen again."

To her credit, Meera's face softened which made him relax slightly. "Never forget the team, Charles," she said. "They pay your extortionate wages after all."

It was more like he paid theirs with the sponsorships and prize money, but even Charles wasn't brave enough to correct her. "I've spoken to Luis and Barnaby," he continued. He'd rehearsed this speech in his head all the way from Harrods. Charm offensives were Charles Worthington's speciality.

"I see you're ahead of me," Meera replied with a wry smile. "I can appreciate that. You must get this rivalry under control, Charles. No one is comparing you to Luis. They're remembering Charles Worthington of two years ago and seeing if you're better. That has to be a yes or we have a problem."

Will, standing behind the laptop, raised his eyebrows. He hated anyone speaking to Charles like this. At the end of the day, Charles had asked for it.

"There will be no further problems," Charles assured her. "I can promise you that." He became aware of Will staring at him intently.

"That's good," Meera replied. "I suggest you spend time today thinking about how you're going to do that."

"In actual fact, Luis is coming over to spend the afternoon," Charles told her proudly.

She raised an eyebrow. "Okay, you've played a blinder on this call. I will share with you that I had it in my mind to fine the fuck out of you."

Charles tried his best not to scoff. She could try. "Give me a chance and I'll prove it to you," he said, earnestly. For once in his life, this wasn't just talk. He genuinely meant it.

"Don't fail the test."

This was his moment to gain some ground and have it out with her. The rage he had felt since Monaco had shown no sign of disappearing. "One other thing," he said ignoring the look of incredulity she adopted.

"Oh, yes? What can I do for you?" Her words positively dripping with sarcasm.

"The bottle of vodka," he said sharply. "Don't do that again. I will not be manipulated like that."

She frowned. "I have no idea what you are talking about."

Charles had been lied to by many people in his life and he'd told his fair share too. Either way, he'd become adept at spotting them, and he believed her confusion. Meera had more confidence than a leopard in a hen coop. She had no reason to cover her tracks.

"Seems Barnaby planted a bottle in my room," Charles told her. "It's not fair, Meera."

Shaking her head, she had the decency to be rattled. "That had nothing to do with me, Charles," she said, quietly. "I will deal with it."

"Then we both have homework."

"You are a cheeky bastard. Win a race or help Luis. Either. That is your homework."

The screen went blank. She did like a dramatic exit.

"You're shagging him," Will declared.

Charles snapped to attention. "Who?"

"Don't give me that," Will replied. "One minute you're scrapping, the next you're all chummy on the plane."

Charles rolled his eyes. "We were not chummy on the plane. Jesus Christ, you see a bit of professionalism and think the worst. You need to see someone."

Will wouldn't be put off. "Bullshit, big brother. You're sleeping with him."

He had never been able to keep anything from Will. Not for long. "Do you think anyone else will twig?" he asked, letting his body relax.

Will came round and ruffled his hair. "Probably not, but you need to be careful. That is a very lucrative story."

Charles got up off the stool he had been sitting on and stretched. He needed a hot shower before Luis came. He would be stinking after his run. "So, what do you suggest?"

"Bang someone else at the same time," Will replied.

The idea of sleeping with anyone else was not on the cards in the slightest. Charles had spent sleepless nights thinking about all the things he had yet to do with Luis. Why on earth would he even contemplate sleeping around? He remembered the trust he found in Luis' eyes. "What if its more than just sex?"

Will looked nervous. "Oh fuck, then we have choppy waters ahead. You fucking idiot."

Shrugging, Charles grabbed an apple from the bowl. "Don't bang the door on your way out," he said, biting into it. "I've got a date to get ready for."

As he made his way up the stairs, Will followed him into the corridor. "Charles," he called after him.

"Yeah?" he said, stopping and looking back.

"Be careful. I like seeing you like this. I don't want to lose you again."

Poor Will had borne the brunt of Charles' bad behaviour and had spent so much energy trying to cover up for him. "I won't," Charles replied gently. "I like it too."

After a long hot shower that pummelled his rapidly seizing muscles, he found himself, once more, standing in his dressing room trying to decide on what to wear for Luis. As he held a shirt up to himself, he caught his stupid grin in the mirror. Will had been right, he must be wearing this like a brand-new tattoo.

In the privacy of his own home, he could do whatever he wanted. He pulled on a pair of navy shorts and matching fitted shirt. With a final glance in the mirror, he knew he looked good. Full of confidence, he made his way downstairs to wait for Luis. Butterflies swirled as he glanced out of the window like a teenager waiting for their prom date.

They had had fun in Monaco but not taken it all the way. Charles desperately wanted to know what it felt like. He'd been out and bought half of Boots' condom aisle. They were all discreetly stashed around the house just in case the mood struck.

A plan had formed last night when he'd been lying awake.

The doorbell sounded through the house and Charles flung the door open to find Luis there. Charles' body gave that familiar jolt that he was starting to really enjoy whenever Luis came in the picture. "Hello," he said.

The shy smile Luis gave made Charles' go weak at the knees. God, this man knew how to push his buttons.

"Hello," Luis replied, strolling into the house.

Charles liked this confident side of Luis. In the press he came across as reserved, so this had been quite a welcome discovery. As the door clicked shut, Luis pushed Charles up against the wall, the spring cold of his body chilling Charles.

They kissed, Charles grabbing the back of Luis' head and holding him close. Luis held on to Charles' waist, grinding his cock against him. It had only been a day, yet Charles' body yearned for this.

Roughly dragging Luis' jacket off, he let it fall to the floor. "Good to see you," he said.

Luis kissed his neck, making him cry out. "Fuck, I've been thinking about this all night," he whispered into Charles' ear.

His accent and low voice always sent ripples of pleasure

through Charles' body when he did that. "I've got plans for you," Charles said. "And they don't involve clothes."

"Is that right?" Luis asked. "Are you asking me to strip at the door?"

"I absolutely am," Charles replied. "And in the interests of good hosting, I'll show you how it's done."

Giggling like teenagers, they threw their clothes off right there in the hallway. Once naked, they fell into each other's arms again. Charles kissed Luis hard, letting his tongue explore his mouth. Their cocks had already come to life. Luis pressed his toned, hard body against Charles'. Once again, Charles drank in his woody scent. He let his hands explore Luis' skin, his fingertips luxuriating in the soft touch.

"Fuck, that feels good," Luis said. "Where's your bedroom?"

"We're not going to the bedroom?"

Luis frowned. "If you've got some kind of dungeon, that isn't my scene."

Charles chuckled and kissed him on the lips. "Never say never," he replied with a wink. "But not today, Luis."

He led him through into the kitchen, Luis grabbed him and pulled his body close. "In the kitchen? Is that hygienic?" he murmured.

Charles wriggled free and opened the door that led down to the sanctuary in the basement. They went down the steps and Luis let out a gasp. It was an impressive space. All the walls were painted dark grey with the pool lit up by lights. The jacuzzi sat to the side along with a four-man sauna.

He had prepared for Luis' coming with towels on the heated recliners and mocktails chilling in a big jug.

"This is incredible," Luis said. Wandering around, he took it all in.

"No one comes down here but me and the cleaner," Charles said, enjoying his reaction. "So, you're very honoured."

Luis dragged his foot along the water. "Nice temperature too."

Charles walked up to him. Luis opened his arms ready to accept the hug. The shock on his face when Charles shoved him hard was priceless. He fell into the pool with a huge splash. The water roiled as though Jaws himself were in there until Luis made it to the surface.

"You evil man," he spluttered.

Laughing, Charles leapt in the pool. When he came up for air, Luis had already wrapped himself around him. They entwined their bodies, wrapping their legs around each other and Charles held Luis as he manoeuvred him to the side and pressed their hard cocks together.

They kissed. To feel Luis' hard wet body against his made Charles want to give himself completely to him. Everything with this man put Charles on a different level of happiness.

"I can see today is going to be fun," Luis said.

"You have no idea."

CHAPTER TWELVE

The heated recliners had been obscenely expensive. Today, Charles thanked his lucky stars he had splashed out on them. Luis lay there like a God, the water still running down his body. "It's amazing down here," he said.

Charles lay on his side, just taking in the handsome man. Reaching across, he ran his finger down his arm. Soft music played from the hidden speakers. His balls were still aching as he gazed hungrily at Luis.

"I can tell you're looking," Luis said even though he had his eyes closed.

"I make no apology," Charles replied, licking his lips. "You're fucking gorgeous."

As if to tantalise him further, Luis stretched his long, lithe body. His cock was semi hard, and Charles almost drooled when he saw Luis' muscles flexing. Unable to contain himself anymore, he leapt off his recliner.

Luis opened his eyes as Charles straddled him.

"I can't host very well if you're all the way over here," Charles said, leaning down and kissing Luis.

Luis ran his hands up Charles' body while Charles ran his through Luis' wet hair. The way Luis kissed him sent him skyrocketing. He would change the tempo all the time, yet it was always what Charles wanted, almost like Luis had a sixth sense.

Charles ground his arse against Luis' solid cock. They had had great sex in Monaco, but what if things were different in his own home? Charles had always been confident of his abilities, but the need to please Luis was all-encompassing and his nerves were threatening to get the better of him.

Moving away, Charles stood, so his cock was inches away from Luis' full lips. Luis licked the tip before opening up and letting Charles slide inside.

"Oh fuck," Charles moaned as the heat from Luis' mouth enveloped his hard dick. He slowly ran his cock in and out of Luis' mouth. Luis controlled him with his hands on his arse cheeks, and Charles stared down at him. "You're fucking perfect," he whispered.

"Show me," Luis pulled his mouth free to reply.

Dropping to his knees, Charles took Luis in his mouth. As he relaxed, Luis ran his hands through Charles' damp curls. The taste of the salty precum made Charles' cock twitch uncontrollably. In the past Charles had been so preoccupied with his own pleasure he had never feasted on a body the way he did with Luis. Every part of him turned Charles on.

Letting Luis' cock fall out of his mouth, he ran his hands up and down his body. Tonight, he wanted to take it to the next level. He stroked Luis' cock and balls. Luis spread his legs, and Charles ran the tip of his finger lightly over Luis' hole.

"I want to fuck you," he murmured.

Luis smiled. "I want to fuck you too."

Charles had always been versatile, but he usually went for top. Well, to be fair, his partners generally wanted to be fucked by a race car driver. It wasn't that he was taken aback by this. When he'd thought about him and Luis together, he'd pictured himself as doing the fucking.

"What's the matter?" Luis asked. "Don't you do that?"

"Yes, I do that," Charles replied. "In fact, I'd do anything with you."

He liked the fact that Luis, the younger and quieter of them, called the shots when he needed to. He found it surprisingly horny.

"Then what are you waiting for?" Luis dared him. "Do you have condoms?"

"Do I have condoms?" Charles laughed. He reached under the heated recliner and produced condoms and lube.

Luis burst into giggles "As if by magic. How did you know you'd make your move here? This feels very scripted."

Charles kissed him. "Between you and me, there are condoms in the lounge, spare room, my room, the kitchen, and even my office. I thought I'd leave it to chance which ones we used."

They both collapsed into fits of hysterics. This was another new thing to Charles, feeling so close to a partner that he could find humour in what was usually a very serious situation.

Luis kissed him. "Honestly, you can fuck me if you prefer. I don't want to make you do something you feel uncomfortable with."

Now that he'd sowed the idea in Charles' mind, he craved it. Ripping the condom wrapper, he pulled it out. Charles took hold of Luis' hard cock. The silky skin felt smooth to his touch.

"He's into it," Luis said.

Charles rolled the condom over Luis. His cock was pretty big, and Charles swallowed hard. This wasn't doing much for his nerves, but his body needed this. He wanted to show Luis that he was serious about them. The new Charles wasn't just a fuck-and-go merchant.

"It's been a while," Charles said, leaning forward and kissing him. "Go gently with me."

Putting his hands behind his head, Luis stared lazily at him. "How about you stay completely in control?"

God he was so fucking hot.

Applying the lube to himself, Charles had to control his excitement. The urgency to take all of Luis inside him was very real. That would not be a good idea, however. He had done that once, when he had first started sleeping with men and the pain had been something he had never forgotten. In fact, he'd leapt off the poor soul beneath him like a scalded cat and refused to continue.

Taking his time, he lowered himself onto Luis' cock. As he let it gently inside him, the fire burned. He wanted this so much. Charles let out a moan.

Reassuringly, Luis rested his hands on Charles' thighs. "Take your time," he murmured.

For a split second, he thought his body wasn't going to cooperate until Luis breached his hole. Charles held his position. He mentally thanked his personal trainer for insisting on all those lunges. The feeling of invasion made Charles panic that he couldn't do this. He'd been with plenty of people who he simply fucked. How did they do it?

Forcing himself to relax, he moved his body down Luis' hard shaft. At last, his body got used to the sensation, his tension replaced with pure pleasure. Staring down at the softness in Luis' eyes, he felt that special connection again. Everything would be all right.

"Fuck," he whispered. "Fuck, that is good."

Luis stroked Charles' cock, but Charles had to bat his hand away. "Not a good idea," he said. Letting out a breath, he reached the base. Luis took hold of his hips and squeezed him. The tenderness coming from this man nearly made Charles cry. It had been a long while since he had had feelings like this.

He gently began to rock, the stimulation from Luis' cock sending jolts of electricity up his spine.

Luis ran his hands up Charles' body, twisting his nipples as Charles rode him hard.

"Oh, yes," Luis gasped.

Never once breaking eye contact with Luis, Charles' movements became more confident. His arse was on fire and he loved it. The basement was always set at a warm heat. Sweat ran down his back as he ground his hips. Charles grabbed hold of Luis' hands, entwining their fingers. His own cock slapped against Luis' stomach as he rode him. He wanted more. He wanted to be fucked hard.

Standing up, he let Luis' cock slip out of him. Instantly, he felt empty. He needed him inside him again and quicky. Charles went over to his abandoned recliner. Getting onto all fours, he turned to Luis. "Fuck me," he instructed.

Luis clearly didn't need asking twice. He leapt off his recliner and positioned himself behind Charles. Now wasn't the time for teasing and Luis plunged inside Charles once more.

"Oh Jesus," Charles cried out. "That's fucking incredible."

Luis slapped his arse cheek and started to pound him. It had been too long since Charles had completely lost connection with reality. All he focused on now was the motion of Luis' body. Gripping the end of the recliner, he spread his legs wide, welcoming every inch of Luis.

"I'm going to come," Luis grunted.

Reaching below him, Charles took hold of his cock. He needed to come while Luis was fucking him. To have both would be more than Charles could imagine. Luis dug his nails into Charles' hips. He wasn't far off.

"Oh, yeah. Come on."

Luis fucked him harder than ever as he chased his own orgasm. The urgency in Charles sent him over the edge too. Tension flooded out of him as he lost control.

"Oh my God," Charles cried out, panting against the

euphoria assaulting his system. That blissful moment where nothing but his own pleasure mattered.

Luis also cried out as his body tensed. "*Fuck*, Charles," he panted, his thrusts becoming more random as they juddered to a halt.

Sweat ran down Charles' back as he stood. His arse was sore, and he loved it.

He kissed Luis hard. When he'd read in books about not being able to have enough of someone, he thought it sentimental claptrap. Now he found not being connected in some way to Luis unbearable. Tying off the condom, he threw it onto the floor.

Luis wrapped his arms around him and hugged him. "That was amazing," he whispered into his ear.

"I'm sweaty," Charles replied.

"So am I," Luis said. He licked the exact spot on Charles' neck that sent him crazy. He had found that place pretty quickly in Monaco.

"Come on," Charles said.

They padded over to the hot tub and got in. The warm water instantly made Charles' muscles relax.

Luis scooted across so he lay in Charles' arms. "As far as hosting goes, you're pretty fucking good."

Charles sniggered and kissed the top of Luis' head, taking in his scent. "Nothing is too much trouble for my guests," he replied.

They lay there in silence for a while, letting the afterglow wash over them. The music took the pressure off from having to speak. Charles realised he felt content. A very new experience for him. It was way too early to see a future with Luis but to be with someone on his level was a brand-new experience and he liked it. "I'm sorry I misjudged Paulo," he said, eventually.

Luis stroked his arm and kissed it. "I don't blame you. Paulo has used unorthodox methods in the past to get his way. I might have defended him, I know. I'm not saying I didn't have doubts."

Charles tensed. "You didn't sound like you did."

Luis shifted in his arms, so he faced him. "I have hidden depths."

Stroking his jaw, Charles studied his face. "I'll have to dig a little deeper to find out what makes Luis Salvatore tick. Is that what you're saying?"

Luis kissed him. "If you want to," he replied.

"I want to," Charles said, squeezing him in a bear hug. "Although..." He hated to bring the real world into this moment, yet he needed to be straight with Luis. The new Charles Worthington did things like that.

"Although what?"

"Will knows."

Luis wriggled out of his arms and sat facing him. "What?"

"Before you get your knickers in a twist, he asked me," Charles said. "I didn't tell him."

Relaxing slightly, Luis frowned. "How did he guess?"

"Knowing me for all my life?"

"I'm surprised Paulo hasn't twigged." Luis settled against Charles, resting his head on his chest.

"I suppose we'll have to be more careful," Charles said. As he said it, he felt a bit sad. His natural reaction would be to tell the world he'd met someone decent. When the press and the public all wanted a piece of it, things could get complicated.

"I suppose," Luis said wistfully.

The moment was shattered by Charles' stomach growling loudly, which made them both laugh. "Sorry," Charles said. "Where are my manners? Are you hungry?"

"I could eat," Luis replied.

Still naked, they dried off from the hot tub and made their way upstairs.

"You're not going to cook like that, are you?" Luis asked

with a twinkle in his eyes. "I don't want you singeing my new toy."

Charles handed him a pizza menu. "I can't do everything," he said with a grin.

"Cop out," Luis said, kissing him.

They dialled in their order and went into the conservatory, collapsing in each other's arms on the sofa. Charles pulled the soft throw over them.

"You can't answer the door like that," Luis said.

"I have an emergency bathrobe. Don't worry."

Luis slipped his hand over Charles' cock.

"Be careful," Charles said. "It won't hide the obvious."

CHAPTER THIRTEEN

Luis and Charles had adopted a professional distance. Charles was proud of his acting abilities. Their week had been busy but even in the midst of it, they shared little smiles that no one could knew were so loaded. Luckily they had a gap until the next race in Azerbaijan. South Tel had them in most days, testing out ideas and strategies for the rest of the season.

Charles seemed to swap between violent ecstasy and desperate craving for more. He didn't know if he would even be able to focus on the racetrack.

"When this driving gig dries up, I might have a go for Hollywood," he said to Luis at dinner that night. "No one has a clue that we're fucking."

At the end of the working day, Charles had jumped at the invitation to Luis' loft apartment. He wondered if Paulo suspected something. Luis had had to meet him for a drink. The wait until the coast was clear had nearly killed Charles.

Luis' home was perfect. Family photos lined every available surface. Brazilian art lined the walls and some incredible smells were coming from the kitchen.

They were sitting on Luis' heated outside patio that overlooked Regent's Park. Smoked glass panelling meant they could see out and that it would be practically impossible for anyone to view them. Even so, Charles didn't like being outdoors. The paparazzi worked wonders with their lenses these days, the public's never-ending appetite for candid shots spurring them on.

"You took things too far when you said I can't grow a beard." Luis pouted.

Charles chuckled. "I was only winding you up."

Luis put down a huge casserole dish out of which some amazing aromas permeated through the spring evening.

"That smells amazing," Charles said. "What is it?"

"It's feijoada," Luis announced proudly. "A Brazilian black bean and meat stew. I thought I'd give you a taste of my past."

The nervous vulnerability on his face made Charles' heart sing. "Thank you," he said, squeezing Luis' leg.

Luis dished up some seriously generous portions. "I can grow a beard," he said, pouting. "In fact, I'll make you feel my stubble on your hole tonight."

Bam. Charles' cock twitched into life.

"These trousers are very tight," Charles said.

"I noticed," Luis retorted.

"Go easy."

Luis put a plate of food in front of him. Charles' couldn't wait to dig in. The first forkful made his tastebuds sing. The cube of pork had been cooked to perfection so it melted in his mouth. But it was the taste of black beans that really came to the fore. "This is good," he said.

"I'm glad you like it," Luis replied with a beam. "I was brought up on it."

Charles raised his glass. "And brought up well."

Silence descended upon the table. Charles took another bite of the delicious food and stared at Luis. "There's something bothering you. What is it?"

Luis instantly put on a fake smile. "No, nothing. Don't be silly."

"*Luis.*"

He sighed. "I don't want to drag you down. It's supposed to be a fun evening."

Taking Luis' hand, Charles leant forward. "Being with you is fun," he said. "I don't just want that though. Talk to me."

Worry had become etched on Luis' face. He took a big swig of his drink. "It's my contract," he said. "Meera called us in this afternoon."

Charles didn't like the sound of this. "Go on."

"She says I've had a shit start to the season compared to last year."

Guilt washed through Charles' system again. What he wouldn't give for a decent glass of wine at that moment. "I wouldn't say shit," he began.

Luis stilled him with a finger on his lips. "Her position is if I don't get a podium win in the next three races, then I should probably be shopping myself around."

Charles was absolutely gutted. He had no idea what this adventure with Luis would result in if anything. He did know that if they were racing in opposing teams, it would kill it stone dead. He did not want that under any circumstances. His mind raced at what to do.

"She's a hard one," he mused. "Fuck it. There are two of us on the track now. If you need a podium win, then we will get you one."

Luis threw himself into Charles' arms. "You are wonderful."

Charles hugged him back. "Did you think I wouldn't help you?"

"I thought after Monaco. Well, bed was bed and track was track."

Charles stroked his cheek. "I was a twat in Monaco. I'm not going to throw myself in front of Jackson Trench's car for you, but if I can help you while I'm going for it, then it's yours."

They kissed. To be in a team, a real team was exhilarating.

"You know the best thing about feijoada?" Luis said.

"What's that?" Charles replied, kissing where Luis' shirt collar opened.

"It can be reheated," Luis whispered. "In case dinner gets interrupted."

Charles kissed him, the taste of the dish still on his lips, and found his way inside Luis' shirt. The soft skin he craved awaited him. "I need you naked," he demanded.

Luis led him through into the apartment. Off the side of the grand lounge lay a huge bedroom with a wooden-panelled wall and grey carpets. Luis had created a sensual space. The bed dominated the room with a velvet teal headboard and crisp white bedding.

Throwing their clothes off, Luis and Charles sank onto the bed. On the way over, Charles had thought about this moment. He had given Luis control up until now. Tonight, he wanted it to be different.

Charles crawled on top of Luis, who wrapped his legs around Charles' waist as they continued to kiss. Charles ran his cock against Luis' hole, grinding his hips. The heat from Luis' body made him hornier than ever—if that were possible.

Once again, Charles smelt Luis. Even that day at the offices, the aroma of him had sent messages to Charles' cock that shouldn't be sent when he had a tight racing suit on. "I've wanted to do this all day," he whispered in Luis' ear.

"Me too."

Charles moved so he could see Luis. "Turn over," he instructed.

Luis did as he was told then settled his body onto the plush duvet, the bright white cotton perfectly framing his honey skin. Charles leant down and kissed the back of his neck.

Sighing a little, Luis got himself comfortable on the pillow.

Gently, Charles traced kisses down Luis' spine. He followed it all the way down until he reached the top of Luis' ass. He had no intention of stopping there though—the taste of him left Charles wanting more. Luis spread his legs wider, giving Charles a green light.

Shifting his position, Charles nipped Luis' ass cheek with his teeth. Just lightly, enough to make Luis squirm.

"Oh yes," he murmured into the pillow.

Charles wanted him to suffer a little longer. He ran his tongue around the top of Luis' thigh. It made Luis shudder. Inches away from the target now, Charles held back. Instead, he licked Luis' other thigh. Once more, Luis tensed.

Burying his face into Luis' ass, Charles licked his hole. This time Luis let out a cry. That was exactly what Charles had wanted. Grabbing Luis' cheeks, he roughly pulled them apart. His hole lay exposed and ready for Charles. Unable to stop, Charles dove back in, his tongue exploring. Luis was writhing with each stroke. It was the most intimate of acts and it turned him on like no other.

Moving a little, Charles rubbed his finger over Luis' tight hole. "I want to fuck you."

"Condoms are in there," Luis replied, gesturing to a bedside cabinet.

Charles continued to probe Luis' ass. He could hardly bring himself to move away to get the condoms. He found them in a scarily ordered drawer next to the lube, all neatly stacked.

Luis got onto his knees and ran his hands down Charles' body, massaging his cock. "How do you want me?" he whispered.

"On your back," Charles replied, kissing him. "I want to see your face."

Once again, Luis settled against the pillows, this time

watching Charles. He was so bloody gorgeous. Charles expertly slid the condom onto his solid cock and positioned himself between Luis' legs. "I am the luckiest man in London, right now," he said, more to himself than Luis.

"More corny lines," Luis said with a groan. "You won't be getting anything if you keep those coming."

Charles leant down and ran his tongue along the silky ridge of Luis' cock. Once more, the salty taste of Luis danced on his tastebuds. Reaching the top, he took him in his mouth. Luis' body relaxed before Charles moved away, letting it fall onto Luis' stomach.

"Less of your lip," Charles ordered, looking up with a smile.

"You win."

Charles applied a liberal amount of lube onto his fingers and pushed them inside Luis. It was tight but he soon found the heat of Luis.

Luis lifted his legs, gripping them with his hands. "Fuck me, Charles."

Once he'd slicked his cock with the rest of the lube, Charles pushed against Luis' ass. He had been thinking about this for days and now he was here, with him, like this, the expectation on Luis' face made him want it all the more. Slowly, he gained access. As the head breached Luis, Charles moaned. The warmth he found there sent waves of pleasure all around his body.

"God, you feel good," he said on a groan. He caught Luis' gaze and the trust he found in it made his heart skip.

Luis bit his lip. "More," he whispered. "I won't break."

Once Charles was fully inside him, Luis' body enveloped him, making his cock tingle. Holding Luis' legs, Charles started to buck his hips, pulling almost the whole way out before plunging back inside. Each time the waves of desire he felt over-whelmed him. "Fuck, this is amazing," he gasped.

Luis lazily stroked his own dick as he stared up at Charles.

"Is that all you got?" He grinned. "I thought you were the best fuck on the circuit."

"You asked for it," Charles replied. Positioning himself so he had more purchase, he fucked Luis harder.

"That's it," Luis coaxed. "Fuck yes."

Knowing he was giving Luis pleasure spurred Charles on. He leant forward to kiss Luis, their chests pressing together, two hearts so close and beating hard. Charles ground his cock in and out of Luis, revelling in every stroke. Luis grabbed his shoulders, digging his fingers in.

"Jesus, Charles," he gasped. "You are amazing."

Charles stopped and spun Luis over. "Kneel up against the headboard," he instructed. "And spread your legs."

Luis obeyed him. As quick as a flash, Charles pushed inside Luis again. Luis cried out, grabbing hold of the headboard. Charles flattened his chest against Luis' back, kissing his neck. He reached around him and grabbed Luis' hands as they fucked. It was raw and primal, and when Luis reached behind, taking hold of Charles' hips, it was as though every part of their bodies had to be touching

"Come for me," Luis grunted.

Roughly, Charles pulled at Luis' body so they both sank on the bed. Luis sat on Charles' cock with his back to him. "Make me," Charles replied, slapping Luis' ass.

Luis took the cue and rode him hard. He held on to the headboard with one hand and pulled at his own cock with the other.

"I'm going to come," Charles cried out. Gripping the sheets, he tensed his whole body as the that blissful release of self-control came. His fingernails dug into the soft flesh of Luis' hips, each wave of pleasure making him see stars.

Luis leant back and cried out. His hole contracted against Charles' cock, making the aftershocks ripple through his body. Charles wrapped his arms around Luis' taut stomach to ground him as the pleasure dominated his body. Eventually, Luis moved away. He took the condom off Charles, tied it, and threw it in the waste bin. "Wow."

They snuggled up on the bed, Charles wrapping his arms around Luis. "Wow, indeed," he replied, nuzzling his hair. "You're so fucking sexy."

The traffic on the London streets below was making a racket. Charles wouldn't have cared if the whole city were on fire. He had found a happy place, and nothing would get a chance to put that at risk.

CHAPTER FOURTEEN

The flight to Azerbaijan had taken off with no incident. The South Tel private jet had been put at their disposal again. This time, however, the cabin was full to bursting.

Barnaby sat at the rear with his assistant. He'd barely said a word to Charles. Presumably Meera had hauled his disgusting arse over the coals. Charles hoped so anyway. He sat facing Will at the front of the cabin. The flight time was five hours and he wanted to get some shut-eye, but it was way too loud for that.

Luis and Paulo were seated in the middle of the craft next to Meera and her husband. She had taken the decision to come to every race for the rest of the season. Charles wondered if her faith in Barnaby had been shattered that much or if she thought her presence would help with the perceived war between her two drivers. If only she knew.

Either way, she wasn't happy about it. Meera dominated in the board room. What did she bring to the track? Charles had spent way too much time on her bad side. They weren't even halfway through his first season and already she had a target on his back. At least he had time to convince her otherwise.

He didn't seem to be the only one preoccupied. Luis kept casting her very nervous glances. Charles made a mental note that he would give Luis some tips on a poker face that night in bed. If she thought she had him on the run contractually, that would only serve to corrode her faith in him more. Meera was a shark. If she smelt fear, she would go in for the kill.

"Are you even listening to me?" Will asked.

Charles snapped out of his thoughts. Will had been banging on about a night out he and his mates had had at a new bar in Central London. It sounded like all the other nights out they'd had over the years and Charles had zoned him out. "No," he replied truthfully.

"Honest," Will said, shaking his head.

"Sorry," Charles continued. "I was just thinking about things."

Luis and Paulo were huddled up together, as thick as thieves. When Charles caught Luis' eye, he'd look away guiltily.

"Things good?" Will asked.

Charles nodded. "Better than a long time."

"Good."

Paulo's shrill laughter filled the cabin. Charles glanced at Meera, who had been nose-deep in her laptop. She glared across at him.

"*Por que você manteve isso em segredo?*" Paulo exclaimed.

"What's that all about?" Charles said. "They never speak in bloody Portuguese."

"They probably think no one else on here speaks it," Will replied with a smug grin on his face.

Charles and Will shared a knowing glance. They had got that badly wrong. Will had been engaged to a Portuguese model about six years ago. As a wildly romantic gesture, he had learnt Portuguese. Sadly, he'd also slept with her best friend...but the thought had been there.

Wordlessly, Will rearranged himself to hear them better.

"*Sinto muito,*" Luis said. "*Precisava ser segredo.*"

Will typed furiously on his phone and held the screen up to Charles.

I'm sorry. We weren't going to tell anyone.

Charles' stomach lurched as though they had hit the worst turbulence.

"*Eu não te culpo.*" Paulo sniffed.

Will quickly typed, then held it up.

I don't blame you.

Charles shook his head. Nasty little toad. It came as little comfort to Charles knowing Paulo would be horrified that his little pet had found his way into Charles' bed.

"*Eu pensei que ele estava tentando flerter para ganhar vantagem,*" Luis urged.

Will did his thing.

Trying to flirt to get the advantage.

He didn't like the direction of this conversation. Half of him wanted to tell Will to stop and the other half desperately wanted to know what they said next.

"*Entao, você foi um melhor,*" Paulo replied.

They both fell about in giggles. God, Paulo annoyed him more than anyone had in a very long time.

"Hey," Meera barked out. "Why don't you kids have some quiet time? The adults are working."

Charles looked to Will who had an expression that Charles didn't like. He held up the phone.

So, you went one better.

It felt as though the pilot had opened up the floor, sending Charles tumbling to the ground. The pity that radiated from Will made things ten times worse.

"Get some sleep," Charles muttered.

Will started to say something and clearly thought better of it. Instead, he put his South Tel eye mask on and got himself comfortable.

Charles took the opportunity to stare out of the window.

The world passed at an impressive rate below but his had spun upside down. Trying to centre his thoughts, Charles broke down his feelings.

Could Luis be doing this for strategy? Charles refused to believe it. He accepted he might not have been the best judge of character over the years, but the thought that he had been wrong about Luis made him want to cry. He had seemed so genuine.

Glancing up, he caught Luis' eye.

Luis gave him a small imperceptible smile. Charles' paranoia had started to grip his insides like a snake. Now he wondered if Luis was smiling at him or himself. Proud that his little scheme had worked, and he'd amused Paulo in the process.

Charles put his own eye mask on.

Suddenly the plane became incredibly claustrophobic. Will had been right. This was supposed to be about his career, not his cock.

Will I ever learn?

Mercifully, when they came to land, things got busy. They were rushed through the airport and did some interviews with local press. Charles fought against his feelings and remained in control even though Luis stood right next to him.

"Charles," Meera said as they waited for their cars. "We have a sponsor drink at six. After that, I want you asleep."

"Yes, Mum," Charles said, with a wink.

Meera shook her head. "I'm not that much older than you, cheeky bastard."

"Sorry," Charles replied. "I guess I'm feeling a little old today."

They both glanced over at Luis and Paulo, who were still

giggling. Charles instantly assumed they were taking the piss out of him.

"Yes," Meera said, lost in her own thoughts. "Then who'd want to learn all those hard lessons again?"

Alarm flashed through his system. Did she really plan on binning Luis? He should warn him against pushing her in that direction. Then he remembered that really wasn't his concern. Luis was an adult. He would have to take care of himself. Charles had races to win.

Riding up in the lift, Will still hadn't wiped that awful pitying expression from his face.

"Please stop." Charles sighed.

"What?"

"That face."

"It's the only one I have, you grumpy twat," Will muttered. "Don't blame me because your dick got you into trouble. How the mighty have fallen."

Charles caught sight of himself in the mirror. He couldn't even defend himself. That was exactly what he had done. "I feel like a prize knob," he said.

Will clapped him on the shoulder. "You're not the first or the last. Don't beat yourself up. Any ideas what you're going to do?"

He had absolutely no answer for that. Charles would not let this season be a failure. Of course, it was too much to hope for that he'd win it. If he brought some points to the team and finished in a respectable place, it would be enough to show Meera his ongoing commitment to South Tel. No matter what Barnaby told her.

"It's all about me now," he said. "Luis might not even be an issue after this season. Meera's turning on him. You know what it's like in this game. When you've lost the CEO, you've lost it all."

Will looked deep in thought. Experience set alarm bells

ringing in Charles' mind. "Whatever is whirling around in that murky little head of yours, get rid of it."

"No idea what you're talking about," Will replied. His attempt at innocence fell very flat.

The lift reached the floor, and they progressed through to the suite. It was decent enough. After years of staying away from home, hotel rooms had merged into one. Huge windows overlooked the city of Baku. Charles had raced here many times and enjoyed the track. "I'm going to get some sleep," he said. "What are you doing?"

"Not sure," Will replied, stretching. "I'll go and find my room. Have a scout around. Anything you need?"

Charles flopped down on the soft couch. "A win here would be pretty fucking spectacular."

"That's down to you," Will replied with a wink.

The door shut behind him and Charles revelled in the solitude. Closing his eyes against the sunshine streaming through the windows, he thought about Luis. There must be more to this than he gave him credit for.

He regretted the way he'd behaved towards him. Even the suggestion that Luis had been leading him on filled him with dread. Perhaps he shouldn't have got involved with anyone. Things were still very early days for Charles. It was a red flag and what kind of driver would he be if he ignored those? Charles thanked his lucky stars that it had come in this form and not something altogether more hurtful.

His phone vibrated on the glass coffee table. Sitting up, Charles saw that it was Luis calling. Unable to face it, he flipped the phone over and ignored it.

He wandered through to the bedroom and flopped down on the white bed. The extra soft duvet welcomed him. He tried to force the image of Luis' naked body underneath it from his mind unsuccessfully. That wouldn't be happening.

He must have dozed off. When he opened his eyes, Will stood over him.

"Come on," he said, breathlessly.

"What? What time is it?"

"You have half an hour to get ready for the drinks. Sponsors, remember?"

"For fuck's sake," Charles groaned. "Coffee. Immediately."

Will trotted off to do his bidding. Charles hated schmoozing almost as much as he hated interviews. They had been fun in the early days but soon lost their appeal. In the old days he would drink his way through them. Dealing with sponsors sober revealed a whole new world of torture.

The scene that awaited him downstairs was one of his worst nightmares. Firstly, he had underdressed in shirt and trousers while everyone else had suits. Even Paulo had one on. Secondly, a sponsor had asked him what his role in the team was. As though Charles were the goddamn floor sweeper. That had been in front of Meera too. Thirdly, Luis kept stalking him like a panther.

His luck ran out as he came out of the bathroom. Luis must have been lying in wait for him and pounced.

"What the fuck is going on?" he blurted out.

Confusion seemed to be coming from his every pore and Charles knew he'd treated him badly. He couldn't bring himself to open up. He had to protect his progress.

"Nothing," he replied. "I just need to focus for the race."

"Too focused for a night-time caller?" Luis asked hopefully.

He wasn't going to make this easy.

"Yes," Charles replied. He hated the way his words sounded so cold but his whole being prevented him from being any other way. "I think perhaps we both need to concentrate on the race and the ones ahead."

Luis took a step back. "Oh, okay. Wow. I wasn't expecting that."

"Luis, listen," Charles replied. Suddenly he felt very tired. "Formula One is a bitch. It doesn't do to form attachments. I stand by what I said. Whatever I can do to help, I will. I need to make a success of this. I'm sorry."

He didn't even wait for Luis' answer. The tears that were bubbling up inside him were threatening full-blown mutiny and he dashed straight out of the lobby. Of course, Will followed hot on his heels.

"Brother," he said when he caught up with him. "What's happening?"

The tears fell out of Charles. Will led him to the far end of the lobby.

"Talk to me," he said.

"I don't know," Charles replied. "I think I just threw away something really fucking good. All because I can't open myself up."

Will took his hand. The earnest expression on his brother's face tugged at Charles' heartstrings even more.

"Charles, listen," he said. "They're two jumped-up little queens. Don't let them get to you. Think about it. Luis needs a podium win. Yes, I know it sounds good to Barnaby and Meera when he says you're a team. I bet he'd jump at the chance to fuck you over with mind games though. You're just one less opponent for him."

That kind of talk put fire in Charles' belly usually and he had to admit there were slightly burning embers. He would need to speak to Luis properly. That would have to wait. He had another goal in mind.

"Then I'll just have to win, won't I?"

CHAPTER FIFTEEN

The next morning, Charles resolved that he would talk to Luis after the qualifiers. It had been ridiculous of him to ghost Luis like that. He had one victory though. He hadn't hit the bottle. In the past he would never get drunk before a race, but a nerve calmer or two had always been on the menu off the track.

However, after a lot of tossing and turning, he'd managed to fall asleep and woken up with a whole new mindset. The two main aims of the day were to finish with a decent starting position for the race and to sort things out with Luis.

When he got down to the pit, it felt as though people were looking at him. He tried to put it down to qualifier nerves. He would speak to his counsellor about this paranoia. They had said his mind might play tricks on him. That withstanding, he could swear people were scowling in his direction.

"Hey, Susan," he shouted over to one of his favourite mechanics.

Weirdly, she just put her head down, seemingly engrossed in checking the tyres on Luis' car.

One of the controllers walked past. "Hey, Paul," Charles said. "What's going on?"

Paul held his hands up. "Keep me out of it, mate." He scurried past, leaving Charles at a loss how to explain this weird reception.

Something caught his eye and there was someone who would hold the answer. Meera stood in the walkway through to the rooms at the rear. The glare coming from her filled him with dread.

"Charles," she shouted. "A word. Now."

Feeling the stares of his colleagues searing into him, Charles walked across the pit area. Meera's face was unreadable as he approached her. He would be prepared to bet his evaporating bonus he was in trouble though.

Charles followed her through to the little rooms. To his surprise, he found a furious Luis, Barnaby and, of course, Paulo waiting for him. The excitement on Paulo's face gave him a code-red alert.

"What's going on?" he asked, glancing from one to the other.

"As if you don't know," Luis replied. "I should knock your fucking block off."

He made a move towards Charles, but Barnaby stopped him with a hand on his chest. "There will be none of that."

"Are you going to enlighten me on what I'm supposed to have done now?" Charles asked Meera with a frown.

Paulo sniggered. If he hadn't been so preoccupied getting to the truth, Charles would have dearly loved to tear a strip off him. He'd keep. "Meera?" he added.

She took a step toward him and really stared into his face. "Are you telling me you have no idea why the pit crew all want your bollocks for Christmas baubles?"

The pit crew? Charles had no idea what their problem was. He'd always made a point, wherever he raced, that he treated the crew with the utmost respect. They were the reason he stood on podiums, and he'd never forgotten that. Not even in the dark times.

Holding his hands up, Charles desperately wanted her to see he was being earnest. "I have absolutely no idea. Please, can you tell me?"

Meera raised an eyebrow at Barnaby and nodded. He took a step forward. "It seems that someone tried to bribe them."

"Someone? Who?" Charles asked. "And why?"

This time Luis did take a step forward. "To bring your car in first. That is fucking underhand, Charles."

Realisation dawned on Charles. Usually, cars were called in to change tyres on a need basis. As a driver, if they called him in first, he had an advantage in getting the most out of new tyres. He had heard of bribes being offered in the past. Pit crews were fiercely professional, however. It would spell absolute disaster if a plan like that backfired. Only a fool would risk that.

"I didn't—" he began, then thought about his conversation with Will the night before. How desperate he had been for a win that weekend to rub Luis' nose in it. *He wouldn't, would he?*

"I didn't have anything to do with that," Charles continued. "You have to believe me. I don't need to bribe people to win."

"I thought I had made my position clear on this rivalry," Meera said, ignoring his pleas. "I am not averse to offering two drivers new contracts for next season, Mr Worthington. You have performance clauses in yours, remember."

Before he made another attempt to persuade her of his innocence, she stalked out of the room. Barnaby gave him a scowl that would sour milk before chasing after her.

That left him and Luis. A few days ago, Charles had thought he had found nirvana in this man's arms. Now he looked as though he could cheerfully wring Charles' neck. "Luis," he said. "I promise on anything you like that I had nothing to do with this."

"Of course not," Paulo chipped in.

Charles had forgotten the little toad was there. "Can you fuck off, Paulo?" Charles asked.

"Hey—" Paulo began

"Leave us," Luis interrupted. "Please, Paulo."

Surprisingly, Paulo didn't take any more persuading and slunk off.

"I think I should probably speak to my brother soon," Charles sighed. "I'm sorry, Luis. Truly."

Luis didn't seem as if he were ready to accept the apology. The qualifiers would begin soon, and Charles didn't want to start the race on these terms.

"As if Will would be capable of thinking up that on his own," Luis said.

"You don't give Will enough credit," Charles replied, rearing up. He had given his side of the story. If Luis refused to accept it, Charles would come out fighting. He didn't know any other way.

"Meaning?"

"Meaning he has a first-class degree in sports science, he won a prize at school for cross-country, and he's almost fluent in Portuguese," Charles explained. "All skills he keeps very well hidden but can be useful from time to time."

It was Luis' turn to look confused now. "I have no idea why you're giving me that oaf's CV. I couldn't care less. Now excuse me. We need to get ready. You might not give a shit. I certainly do."

He made to leave but Charles held him by the top of the arm. "He speaks enough Portuguese to understand yours and Maleficent out there's conversation on the plane," he said through gritted teeth.

"I have no idea what you are babbling on about," Luis replied. "If you are trying to distract from your pathetic games, it isn't working."

Charles glared into his eyes. "You 'went one better', did you? My, how you both laughed."

He didn't wait for Luis' reaction. The room suddenly became too hot and overcrowded with the both of them in it, so instead, Charles stormed out to find one of the assistants waiting nervously for him in his changing area.

"What now?" he said with a sigh.

"Your brother is outside," she said. "It seems Meera has banned him from coming in."

Charles sank down on the chair. "Then he's banned. Tell him I'll see him later."

She nodded and scuttled off. Will would be panicking right now if he thought his stupid little scheme had come to light. *Tough.*

Will tended to do ridiculous things but he had surpassed himself this time. He might have ruined Charles' career in one move. It wasn't confirmed yet that he hadn't.

Closing his eyes, he tried to think about the meditation exercises they had taught him at rehab. It had all been about shutting the outside noise down. How the fuck was he supposed to do that and focus on a race when all this drama seemed to be constantly raging?

"I don't give a fuck what he said. Get out of my way."

The dulcet tones of Hilary rang through the place like a screeching raven. Charles gave up on finding his zen and got to his feet.

An irate Hilary appeared.

"When did you get here?" Charles asked. "Bloody hell, Hil. You pop up at the weirdest moments."

She stormed over to him. "I had brought the hubby here for a birthday treat," she growled. "Instead, I've had to come down here and see what the fuck you're playing at."

"I'm just about to walk to the car," Charles said. "It would be nice to have a bit of focus time."

"You can focus on my words, you stupid fuck. What the hell is this about bribes?"

Surely Meera or even Barnaby hadn't blabbed to her already. Even for Hilary, she had found out in record time.

"It's a misunderstanding. How do you know about it anyway?"

"Because Ray Spencer from *The Sun* has been on the blower asking me about them."

It had been twenty minutes since his dressing down. Admittedly, in this age of communication, stories were broken in less time. They usually had help from someone on the inside, though. "Where did he get it from?" Charles demanded.

"As if he'd tell me. He seemed pretty sure of it."

Charles scrubbed his face. Everything piled on top of him and at the worst possible time. "Truth?" he said. "Will has been an idiot and tried to put the boot in to Luis."

Hilary let out a sigh. "I only hope that brother of yours has a big dick because you took the looks and the brains from your particular gene pool. What the fuck?"

"I know," Charles replied. "I haven't had a chance to speak to him yet. Luis is pissed off and rightly so. I can't believe he would go straight to the tabloids though. Surely not?"

Hilary narrowed her eyes. "You leave this to me. Ray Spencer and I once had, shall we say...a moment on a barge on the Thames."

Charles shuddered. On top of everything else, he did not need the mental image of Hilary having a knee trembler along London's riverway.

"I've already killed the story for now," she said. "I'll find out who it came from and discredit the shit out of them. They're fucking with the wrong people."

When the chips were down, having Hilary on his side was worth a hundred other people. Her reputation for hard dealing made editors shudder. Her client roster contained more stars than the Milky Way. If she boycotted a publication, they felt it immediately.

"Thank you, Hilary. I mean it," he said, hugging her. "I'm a twat but I'm a principled one."

"Just go and win that qualifier," she said.

He would do better than that. He would win the whole bloody Grand Prix.

~

"How many laps to go?" Charles barked into his headset.

"Five," his controller replied.

The weekend couldn't have gone better. Once Hilary had left him alone, he had managed to channel all the stress and all the rage into the cockpit and ended up with a second-place start.

Jackson Trench had been in pole. Charles had managed to take him early on. Now he had to defend his lead. "Where's Luis?" he asked.

"Fourth," came the reply. "It's close."

Kim Hak, one of Charles' previous teammates, was third and would be as keen as anyone to knock Charles off the top podium. They hadn't always seen eye to eye, to put it mildly.

He came round the corner tight. The smell of the fuel and the roar of the crowd seemed miles away. All Charles concentrated on was bringing this baby over the line.

The last few laps of a race were critical. Jackson was like a hyena snapping at his legs. Charles had driven against Jackson before and studied the races he hadn't. He knew all his moves and read them like a book.

If Jackson went to the left, Charles blocked him. If he lurched to the right, Charles was there. Often journalists had asked how he seemed to know people's decisions before they did. He assured them that drivers weren't all that different.

There were only so many options on the circuit that he often got lucky.

Really it took a little more skill than that. He had spent years studying the techniques of his fellow drivers. Jackson was always aggressive. His preferred method to barge his way past had served him well to this point. Kim would be wanting to use this dogfight as cover and zoom past both of them. Charles had to be on his guard for either eventuality.

The adrenaline that shot through his system was way more addictive than vodka or cocaine.

"That's four laps, Charles," his controller informed him.

"Status?" he replied.

"Good. Jackson is contained. Luis is battling Kim. The rest, miles behind."

If Luis got past Kim, they would both have a podium win. That should put a smile on Meera's face. As he zoomed around the course, a warning alarm sounded.

Fuck.

"What is it?" he asked.

"Something to do with power," came the reply.

"Can we finish?"

He didn't even try to hide the desperation in his voice. He had almost grabbed victory.

"Keep pushing."

Flooring it, Charles expertly manoeuvred the vehicle around the course. However, it became more of a struggle to get the performance out of the car. As if sensing it, Jackson became more antagonistic. One minute he appeared on Charles' right, the next his left.

"Two laps."

He would not let him through, yet the car was clearly dying. His speed had dropped. As he defended so expertly, Jackson had to brake too, something that would be making him scream blue murder no doubt.

"Status," he demanded.

"Luis is past Kim and on Jackson's ass."

"I'm not going to hold Jackson much longer."

They sped through the course.

"Final lap, Charles."

Charles had a choice. He could let the car go, knowing he had done his best or he could do the right thing. It was now or never. "Tell Luis on the straight. I'll leave the right open."

"Roger that."

Into the final sector and Charles tried everything to get power out of the car, but the gauges were telling him his chances were dwindling. Jackson was on him like he had been all lap. Charles resolutely would not let him pass.

They rounded the slight bend and onto the straight leading to the chequered flag. Charles feinted to the right then swung to the left. Jackson fell for his trick and had to brake to avoid going into the back of him.

At the same time, Luis zoomed past him on the right. Charles gave out a whoop as he saw Luis go over the finish line. He followed closely then Jackson.

They had both won the podium.

Fuck that felt good.

CHAPTER SIXTEEN

The crowd cheered frantically as the top three of the race stood at the side of the stage, ready to take their places on the podium. Luis beamed from ear to ear and waved frantically. Charles caught his eye and winked.

God why did he feel like Han Solo at the end of *Star Wars*? Well, if that made him the older sexier scoundrel, that wasn't so bad. He had been cast as worse in his time. Poor Jackson having to settle for the third stoop glared at Charles as though he wanted to rip him apart. That made the whole thing far sweeter.

"That was very clever driving," he said between gritted teeth. "I suppose you think Meera will fuck you now you've landed one and two slots?"

For a while there Charles had forgotten his public persona. He'd actually got used to talking about himself honestly, if only with Luis and Will. Even so, Charles would not miss the opportunity to really twist the knife.

"How do you know it wasn't a thank-you present?" he replied, flashing his impossibly white teeth at Jackson.

God, he hated him.

Mercifully, they were led up to take their positions. Luis

still waved as though he were a member of The Beatles. It warmed Charles' cynical heart to see the sheer joy on the guy's face.

Each time they locked eyes, the world danced. It became infectious and before he realised it, he was waving and throwing autographed pictures to the crowd too. He did draw the line at the champagne bit though. He felt a bit awkward taking a step away. When the crowd surged into rapturous applause, he openly shed a tear.

Things were feeling very different to Charles Worthington. It both excited and terrified him.

Watching Luis and Jackson drench themselves in champagne, Charles realised how stupid he had been, letting things fuck up so easily. When would he learn to be an adult and talk to people instead of grand gestures?

Then he remembered he had to speak to Will straight after this.

Pop went the bubble.

As soon as possible, he got out of there. It wasn't a quick mission with countless media interviews and people to schmooze.

He made it to the corridor eventually. They let him go on the proviso he would make an appearance in the hotel lounge that evening. He would have to see how the next hour panned out before he dared commit to anything like that.

Checking his phone, it appeared Will had gone to the hotel after the race. In the car on the way there, Charles messaged to find out if he were still there.

It was an affirmative. Nothing more, nothing less.

Tears threatened to come as he sat in the back seat. He tried to put it down to post-race comedown, but inside he knew that he would have to make a really tough call. Twenty minutes later and wrapped in one of the hotel's gorgeous bathrobes, he sat across the couch from his brother.

"Charles..."

He held his hand up. "Honestly, Will, save it. Bribes? What the fuck were you thinking?"

To his credit, Will looked absolutely devastated. "I know. I feel like such an arsehole. I had a couple of drinks in the bar after I'd left you and they were in there. It just seemed like the perfect solution."

Charles rubbed his eyes. The comedown from the race was kicking in and he needed to just be still. "I don't want this to go on," he began. "I'm sorry, Will."

The colour absolutely drained from Will's face. "What?"

"It's a different era now, Will." Fatigue had begun to take a hold of him. He loved to race cars. When had that become swallowed up by all the other shit of politics and sponsors and image?

"And I'm surplus to requirements?" Will retaliated.

He had a right to be worried about his future.

"Don't be so ridiculous," Charles said. "Let's face it, I'm coming to the end of my career. I only really came back to prove I could. I'll see next season out and I can't see anyone else going for it."

Will frowned. "And?"

"I don't need an assistant round here anymore. I've done this shit for fifteen years," he said. "Let's face it, most of the time it was to keep you on the payroll so we could go on the lash."

Will sniggered. "We had fun though, didn't we?"

"We did," Charles replied. "It's gone now. Surely you feel it too."

"I suppose I do," Will said, sadly.

"So, I want to look forward. I would like that to mean you spending the next eighteen months investigating everything that's available. I've signed with HVP Management. I thought you might work with them while I focus on squeezing every last drop out of this shower of bastards."

To Charles' relief, a grin spread across Will's face. "Like a kind of scouting mission?" he said.

"Exactly like that."

Will stood up and practically dragged Charles to his feet. He hugged him hard. "I thought you were going to fire me after all that shit," he said with a huge sob. "I'm so sorry. Sometimes I get carried away."

No shit. Charles wriggled out of his grasp. "Do me a favour. Do not piss HVP off. They are big league. Don't do anything until you speak to me. I am not, repeat not, a silent partner in my own career. I mean it."

Will held his hands up. "You have my word, brother. I'd better go and pack. We have an early call tomorrow." He backed out of the room. At the door he stopped. "You know, Charles," he said. "I only do it for you."

It was a blatant lie but touched him, nonetheless. "Too corny," he replied. "Go and make money."

Will closed the door behind him and Charles let out a huge sigh. The idea had come to him as he'd sat in the cockpit waiting for the start of the race. He'd felt ill at the prospect of sacking him. Will could be HVP's problem. They were making enough out of Charles to add nursemaids to their contract.

Now he would usually have a glass of something to celebrate.

Fucking hell, being sober is boring as fuck.

The exhilaration of the race and the dread of dealing with Will left him vulnerable. It would be so easy to have a cheeky drink in a hotel too. He would not play into Barnaby and Paulo's hands though. Pushing the thoughts from his mind, he went through to the bedroom. The valet had laid out trousers and a shirt, for the drinks.

Faced with the choice of pacing the suite hoping the cravings went away or at least talking to someone to take his mind off things, he got dressed.

When he'd walked in, everyone had insisted on shaking his hand. It soon became evident people were in the mood to party hard. The nonsense that Will had created the day before had been mercifully forgotten.

"Well done today."

Silently, Meera had joined him. She glowed in a bright white dress with her hair swept up.

"Meera," he said, kissing her. "As stunning as ever."

"I treated myself this afternoon," she replied. "You earned me a good bonus today, my friend."

"I trust you will be sharing those spoils with your two glorious drivers."

She took a sip from her champagne. He would bet no one in her life spoke to her like that.

"I might just do that," she replied. "For your cheek."

He had no idea what it was about this woman. She made him go weak at the knees and not in a sexual way.

Oh God, I'm having my first gay girl crush.

He chuckled to himself and instantly wanted to tell Luis. But he sat on the other side of the room holding court with a seemingly endless supply of people hanging on to his every word.

"Something amusing you?" Meera asked.

"Oh, you know me," Charles replied. "Always happy."

Meera frowned. "Is everything all right? I don't do the mushy stuff and please don't tell me anything about your personal life. Fundamentally, you're okay, though?"

Her sheer awkwardness made him burst out into fits of laughter. This only served to make her look like she wanted to crawl out of her own skin.

"Fucking hell, Meera," he said, wiping his eye. "Don't ever go into HR. That was absolutely atrocious."

"Oh, shut the fuck up," she said with a smile. "I can't do all that shit. I don't wish ill on any of you, but I also don't really care what the fuck you've got going on."

This only served to make him double up again. God, it felt good to just laugh. "You've helped me ten times more than hand-holding would have. Thank you."

She seemed relieved the conversation was at an end. "Here to help. Right, I'd better schmooze."

To his relief she floated off to strike fear in the heart of random workers.

Once she'd gone, he realised this was one of the only times he'd gone to something like this alone. He had always had Will to rely on. He would still be in the hotel. Charles contemplated inviting him for pizza in his room. Something stopped him. He'd made it clear those days had ended. Charles had to respect his own decision and be a brave boy on flying solo.

He also worked the room for a while, chatting to crew members. The whole time, he never took his eyes off Luis. He had come right out of his shell. Paulo was at his side, beaming as though he were the one who'd orchestrated Luis' win, not Charles. About an hour into things, Charles decided to call it a night. Hopefully he would crash out before any cravings returned.

Draining his glass, he made his way for the door. As if from nowhere, Luis appeared.

"And where the fuck do you think you're going?" he asked, folding his arms.

"Time for bed," Charles replied. "It's your victory. Go and enjoy it."

Luis grinned. "It's boring as fuck. They just want to talk about race cars. What are you doing?"

"Pizza and a movie. Rock-and-roll race car driver."

Pondering him for a second, Luis nodded. "Yeah, I'm up for

that. Give me ten minutes to slide by my room and change. Pyjamas for pizza, right?"

"I don't remember inviting you," Charles replied unable to quell the feelings of hope inside him.

"I don't remember asking you to," Luis said with a chuckle. That boyish smile was too much for Charles to resist. "Don't be a baby."

Charles wanted this more than anything in the whole world. "You're on."

The sexual tension in the lift as they stepped in could have been sliced up and served on toast. Charles had to keep telling himself he might be reading this completely wrong. Perhaps Luis did just want to hang out.

Even so, he raced through the suite like a cyclone, tidying and checking his hair. He threw his grey pyjamas on. Glancing at himself in the mirror, he did look good. The new glow to his skin made him proud. God, he had earned that.

Just as he stuffed his dirty boxer shorts under a cushion, there came a knock on the door. He dashed over and was greeted by a ridiculously gorgeous Luis. He had on figure-hugging black cotton pyjamas. They gave Charles the perfect view of what he was now missing out on.

He'd laid out an ice bucket with a bottle of fizzy water in. If he had to drown in the stuff, he would do it in style.

"I'm still buzzing after today," Luis said, curling up on the sofa.

"I know," Charles said. "We make a good team when we try."

Luis held his gaze. "Well, I thought so. When you didn't even give me a chance to explain my comments on the whole pit business..."

Charles sank down on the other end of the huge brocade sofa. The opulence in this suite was off the scale.

"That I had nothing to do with, thank you," he interjected. "Don't you dare say you still think I did."

Things maybe taking a turn that he hadn't predicted. He wasn't going to sit there and take the blame for someone else though. Especially not his stupid brother.

"Calm yourself," Luis replied. "I never said that. I do blame you for not giving me the chance to talk to you."

Bull's-eye. Charles had behaved badly doing that. Fuck, he was good. "Fine," Charles said. He had had enough of squabbling. "The floor is yours."

"It won't even sound funny when I tell you. It's just one of those things," Luis explained. "Ever since we were kids, we thought we were so funny to say 'we go one better'. It's really dorky, but if Madonna toured, we got to the front, or if when we were visiting a city for the first time, we'd research all the best places."

The blush that stole over his face made Charles want to reach out to reassure him.

"I told you it was nerdy."

Charles rubbed his eyes. "What a dick I've been." He meant it too. The shame that he hadn't been able to leave his pride behind when he made the decision to go sober stung.

"In all seriousness," Luis said, reaching out for Charles' hand, "I do have feelings for you, Charles. I don't know what that means but I can't and won't deny it."

Boom.

He absolutely had not expected to hear those words come from Luis' mouth. That level of honesty used to make Charles put his running shoes on. Coming from Luis, it pushed him seriously close to crying. Which would be a complete embarrassment.

"Are you going to leave me hanging?" Luis said.

Charles leant forward and kissed Luis so lightly on the lips he could barely feel it. Leaning back slightly, he stared into Luis' eyes. "I'm going to show you," he murmured. "Because you are with the king of going one better."

CHAPTER SEVENTEEN

Luis came out of the bathroom. God, he looked good naked. It might have only been a few days, but Charles hated how he'd come close to losing this. As Luis got on the bed, Charles opened his arms. Luis eagerly snuggled into him and planted a kiss on his shoulder.

"This is nicer than last night," Luis said. He ran his hands over Charles' body.

Charles entwined his fingers in Luis'. "What happened last night?"

"Oh, you know. Worrying myself to sleep. Wondering why I wasn't in here with you. That kind of thing."

Guilty, Charles kissed him. He had promised to show Luis his feelings through actions, and he was absolutely determined to do that. "I'm sorry," he murmured into Luis' neck. "Can we move on? It's been another fucking crazy day."

"Poor baby," Luis whispered in his ear. "Perhaps you'd rather get an early night. I don't want to keep you up."

At risk of being incredibly corny, Charles jacked his own cock and replied, "Bit late for that."

They kissed once more. Charles didn't think he would ever get used to Luis' kisses. They set his lips tingling and his heart soaring. Slowly, he crawled on top of Luis without breaking the kiss. Their cocks ground together as Luis wrapped his legs around Charles' waist.

Feeling Luis grab the back of his head and elevate the kiss made Charles even hornier. They clashed tongues. Charles ran his hands up Luis' arms, pinning them above his head. He licked his armpits, making him squirm.

Their usual brand of slow and sensual lovemaking had been replaced by urgency. He wanted to explore every inch of Luis' body as though he were staking his claim all over again, even though they'd only spent a couple of nights apart.

He started to plant tiny kisses on Luis' neck. Charles revelled in the fact he was having this effect on Luis. Making his way down his body, he traced circles around Luis' nipples with his tongue. When he reached his waist, he kissed the tip of his solid cock. The taste of Luis filled his mouth. God this man did things to him.

Hornier than he'd ever remembered being, Charles focused solely on Luis' pleasure. He licked the end, loving that familiar salty taste. Luis groaned as Charles went to work, each one of those little sounds spurring him on. His own cock ached but he could wait.

Charles stared up at Luis, who had his eyes closed. Charles took his whole cock in his mouth, sliding up and down his shaft.

"Oh, yes," Luis murmured.

Charles couldn't get enough of him. The musky smell of him and the soft touch of his skin all combined made Charles want him so badly. Letting Luis' cock fall out of his mouth, he spread Luis' legs, leaving his hole exposed. Diving for it, he licked furiously. Luis arched his back and gripped the pillows.

"Jesus, Charles," he cried.

Charles planted little kisses up the inside of Luis' thigh before crawling up his body. Luis rolled him over, never breaking the kiss. Taking hold of Charles' cock, he pulled needily.

"Want you to come," Luis whispered.

"Together?" Charles replied.

He reached for Luis' cock. They kissed harder than ever as they took each other to that point of oblivion. Charles was first, his orgasm coming from nowhere. "I'm going to..." Throwing his head back, he cried out, coming in thick spurts over Luis' hand. Luis bit at his neck.

"Oh fuck," Luis exclaimed. He came too, his hand gripping Charles' shoulder as the hot liquid filled his hands.

When they had returned to earth, Luis stared into his eyes. "It's nice to be back in business," he said, nuzzling into Charles' neck.

"And that was better than a handshake."

Luis sprang off Charles and got a towel from the en-suite. He cleaned himself up and threw it to Charles.

"It's crazy," Charles said. "It's only been a day and I've missed you."

Luis sank onto the bed and into Charles' arms. "Me too."

Lying in the bed with just a sheet covering them, Charles couldn't remember being this happy.

"What time is the flight home?" Luis asked lazily.

"Not until ten," Charles replied, nuzzling into Luis' hair. That musky scent again made Charles drink it in.

"Are we off tomorrow?" Luis continued. "How about a lazy night in front of a movie?"

Charles squeezed him tighter. It made his heart soar that Luis wanted to make plans together. Like being a normal couple. "Have you forgotten?" Charles chuckled.

"Forgotten what?" Luis asked with a face of confusion.

Leaning forward, Charles kissed him. He couldn't possibly resist someone as cute as Luis.

Oh God, what is he turning me into?

"We have that competition winner things tomorrow night."

Luis sank into the pillow. "Oh, fuck. I didn't read the email. Paulo mentioned something about it."

The name still made Charles bristle. He did his best to hide it.

"Where is it?" Luis continued. "I don't suppose it's afternoon tea at Claridge's."

Bursting out laughing at the optimism in his voice, Charles took hold of his hand. "Sorry to piss on your chips," he said. "It's a crappo burger place in Piccadilly."

Luis shuddered. "Can't we relocate to Claridge's?"

"I don't think that's possible. What is your obsession with that place anyway?"

Snuggling into his side, Luis stroked Charles' arm. "When I first came to England, I walked past it," he explained. "I'd only really begun so didn't have the spare cash I do now. I vowed to myself, when I met a really decent man, we would go there for afternoon tea like a proper couple."

"That's sweet," Charles replied. "And have you been?"

Luis shook his head. "I never found a decent man."

Charles would give anything to be that man. Things were so up in the air at the moment that he didn't dare get heavy by voicing it. "We should get some sleep," he said, instead.

It sounded like such a lame response, but the moment had passed now. Luis shifted over and Charles moulded his body against him. It had been a long time since Charles had experienced safety like this.

The last thing he remembered before drifting off to sleep was the scent of Luis.

.

~

The jet home gave them a subdued experience. Will had flown separately. Charles absolutely refused to deal with Meera and Will in such a small space for five hours.

He and Luis sat together, which raised eyebrows.

"That's what I like to see," Meera said, sliding into the seats opposite them. "No more talk of this bloody rivalry."

Paulo sat at a table on his own and scowled across at them.

"Are you coming to this event?" Luis asked.

"Burgers and milkshakes?" Meera replied. "Not exactly my favourite but anything for my boys."

Luis sighed. "I hate PR."

"I would have thought Nihal Varma might have come up with something a bit more exciting," Charles added.

Hilary might be old-school, but she had brilliant ideas. A chain burger joint would be very low on her list. People still talked about the time Charles joined the Synergy Studios team. They were sponsoring a huge new theme park in New Orleans, and Hilary had thought it would be a good idea for him to ride every rollercoaster in a day. She had arranged for film crews to follow proceedings and journalists to accompany him on the rides. Sadly, she hadn't allowed for him being sick in front of the world's press. That had been quite the story.

Maybe burgers and shakes were better.

A car had been booked for when they landed, to whisk them off to Central London. Paulo and Luis had got in the first car with Barnaby and one of his assistants. Charles had got in the second with Meera and her husband, Harry.

It felt empty without Will by his side. He stared out of the window.

"Penny for them?" Meera stared kindly at him.

"They're not worth that," he replied. "Just feels a bit odd without Will."

She sighed. "I'm sorry for what happened."

Snapping fully to attention, Charles met her steely gaze.

"He was a dick and deserved it," he said. "Times change. He's quite happy going off and finding the next adventure for us when this dries up."

He caught the look shared between Meera and Harry.

"Are you talking retirement?" Harry asked.

"No." Charles grinned. "Don't panic. This is purely investigation. I've a few years in me yet."

Meera visibly relaxed. "Good, because we're spending a fucking fortune on you."

The car carried them through the London streets. Charles loved his city. He had driven for teams all over the world, but he had refused to live anywhere else.

"Is it just Will that's bothering you?" Meera asked.

He so desperately wanted to say, *"No I'm fucking Luis and I don't know where I stand."* Her face would be a picture. At least she couldn't accuse him of silly rivalry anymore.

"Tired," he said. "I didn't get much sleep last night."

Visions of Luis naked, writhing around his bed, dropped into his mind and his cock gave a twitch. God he couldn't wait to get this bloody engagement over and hopefully have a repeat of last night. All night.

"Me neither," Meera replied.

Once more he caught a silent and knowing exchange between Meera and Harry. Now that was something he absolutely did not want to discuss.

Thankfully, they arrived at Piccadilly Circus before things got too uncomfortable.

A few fans and photographers were outside. Of course, Luis signed everything put out for him, taking his time to dedicate each autograph and posing for endless selfies.

Charles got out of the car and a couple of girls screamed. He grinned. Sometimes, in the bubble of Formula One, he forgot how much it meant to people. It was good to have these events to remember. He joined Luis at the barriers and signed as much as possible.

"You're making them happy," Luis said.

He had a twinkle in his eye that made Charles want to scoop him up in his arms. Instead, he jostled Luis, really for a reason to touch him. "Coming through," he said with a laugh.

Luis pressed against him, and they shared a glance. It was fleeting and no one else would have noticed, but Charles' whole body tingled.

God this man had power over him.

"Right, we will have time for signing after."

Hilary appeared amongst them, resplendent in jeans and a crisp white shirt. She had her ever-present aviator sunglasses on her head and a clipboard. Nobody brandished a clipboard quite like Hilary.

"Lead on," Charles said.

He clapped Luis on the shoulder, and they followed her into an impossibly bright, horribly plastic burger joint. He would have to run for hours on the treadmill to get rid of these calories but once in a while wouldn't hurt.

"Luis. You're over there," Hilary barked.

Two boys and a girl sat eagerly at a table. Luis clapped his hands together and went to join them. Their grins went on for miles.

"As for you," Hilary continued, "I need a word."

That never meant anything good. She led him to the side.

"What's up?" he asked. "Don't tell me no one wants to sit with me. I'm not that bad an eater."

"Don't worry, I have your little darlings over there." She pointed to a table where three girls were scowling at him. Doing things like this always made him nervous. He could drive for hours at super-high speeds but talking to kids was a skill he needed to hone.

"What do I say?" he asked.

"How the fuck do I know?" she replied. "Ask them about school or something. Anyway, listen. My contact came back to me. Guess who fed them the story about Will."

Charles frowned. "Who?"

He followed Hilary's gaze. Paulo sat at the counter with a glass of something, scrolling intently on his phone.

"That little shit," Charles said under his breath.

"Indeed," she replied. "Don't make a scene here. The rest is up to you."

Luis and Charles had decided they would keep a distance from each other. It would only take one switched-on paparazzi and their lives wouldn't be their own.

Inwardly seething, he went and sat at his table.

"Who are you?" one of the girls asked.

Great start.

Once he'd explained who he was and assured them he wasn't some random trying to meet the great Luis Salvatore, they begrudgingly accepted his presence.

After twenty minutes of almost silent munching on burger and fries, they were swapping tables, much to the relief of his little party who were still staring at him, full of distrust.

Paulo had grabbed Luis and whispered something in his ear. Charles took the opportunity to nip to the bathroom. As he walked past them, Paulo instantly stopped talking.

"Don't let me stop you," he said. "My interpreter isn't here today."

Paulo adopted his usual scowl. "And why is that?"

"Enough," Luis said, warningly.

"Oh, you know what it's like," Charles said. "People who don't have the actual skills to win races can sometimes get a bit carried away."

A look of amusement crossed Paulo's face. "That's a strange way to describe your brother."

Charles glanced at Luis who always seemed to be full of

nervous dread when he and Paulo were together. "He's not in my good books," he replied. "I used to think it made everything all right, having him by my side. It's quite freeing to be on my own."

Unsurprisingly, Paulo wasn't up for having a nice conversation. "Even so, family dinners will be interesting," he said. "Have you told Mummy and Daddy that you fired him?"

"Fired him?" Charles said. "I haven't done that. You will have to get your facts straight. Now that you're going into journalism." To his glee, the colour did drain slightly from Paulo's face.

"Paulo?" Luis asked.

"Have you had a relapse or something?" Paulo asked. "You're not making a lot of sense."

Shaking his head, Charles would not have this conversation here. "I've got to finish off some cold fries," he replied. "Listen to me, Paulo. The game is up. I'm not even giving you a warning. You've fucked with me, and I will not forget it."

As he took his seat with his next gang of primary school dinner dates, he searched the room. Paulo was bright red and Luis seemed to be talking to him aggressively. Revenge was a dish best served cold, unlike the congealed fries that lay before him.

"Did you get to meet Luis too?" a little boy asked him.

Charles sighed. "Yeah, I did. Lucky me, eh?"

CHAPTER EIGHTEEN

Luis led them into his apartment. It had been a quiet taxi ride over. Paulo had had a mix of hatred and fear on his face, and Charles had quite enjoyed leaving him dangling. He'd tried to initiate conversation on more than one occasion, but Charles had gleefully told him that anything overheard could become a news story. Paulo had made enough trouble for him that Charles would allow himself a little joy at his discomfort.

"Right," Paulo said. "No one can overhear us now. Out with it."

"Paulo," Luis chided. "There's no need for attitude. Charles, what is going on?"

Sitting down on the vast couch, Charles glared at Paulo. He knew exactly what he had been up to and had chosen aggression as the best form of defence. "Why don't you think about what you've done recently," Charles said. "Or is it too difficult to narrow down?"

Paulo sighed. "Either speak or don't. I couldn't care less."

Luis looked as though he were about to lose his temper. He stalked over to the huge windows that overlooked night-time London. "One of you please tell me what the fuck is going on."

"Fine," Paulo said, dashing forth. "It's obvious he's trying to get in between us. Just because his little brother had to be sent home, he doesn't want you to have me. I suppose he thinks his magical cock is enough."

Charles reared up at this comment. "You can't help yourself, can you?"

"I've had enough," Luis said. "Charles, whatever you're accusing Paulo of, just spit it out."

Getting comfortable on the couch, he stared Paulo straight in the eye. "Okay, I have it on very good authority that this little fuck was the one who sold the story about Will and the pit crew."

The silence that followed told him all he needed to know. Paulo went very red around the neck, his eyes flitting from one to the other.

"Paulo?" Luis asked.

"How ridiculous," he managed. "For what possible reason? I certainly don't need the money."

He was obviously lying. Charles only hoped that Luis wouldn't be fooled by this frankly substandard performance. However Luis had a blind spot to this revolting creature.

"No but it would help if I got into ten tons of shit while Luis contract was being negotiated," he replied. "Meera was bluffing when she said she'd get rid of both of us. Were you in on it too?"

"How could you even think that?" a shocked Luis exclaimed.

Charles didn't really think Luis would be involved. He valued his halo way too much to play dirty like that.

"Have you any evidence for this slur?" Paulo interrupted.

"I can get it," Charles replied. "If you're not going to do the decent thing and own up."

A nasty expression appeared on Paulo's face. "Oh, I see. This is from your own personal rottweiler, Hilary, isn't it? No doubt she's got one of her reporter friends to step up."

Charles turned to Luis. "I don't think Meera would be happy that secrets are being peddled to the highest bidder."

They all knew that Meera would absolutely hit the roof. Luis might have got his podium win, but his contract had not been signed yet.

"Paulo," Luis said. "If you have done this, I want you to be honest."

Charles almost felt sorry for him if he wasn't such a nasty little swine. He was caught in a noose of his own making. To his amazement, Paulo sank down on the chair.

"Fine," he said. "I did sell a story. I didn't do it for the money. I did it for you. If that waste of space got binned, it would be open for you. I only ever do these things for you, Luis."

"You're lucky to have such a loyal friend," Charles replied, drily.

"I don't know why I am getting grief." Paulo sneered in return. "It was your brother who tried to make the bribe."

Charles sat on the couch and stretched his legs out. "Nice try at deflection, Paulo. All that has been dealt with. We're talking about you today."

"Luis," Paulo said. "Why don't you get rid of him, and we can talk."

"I don't think so," Luis said. "Answer me, honestly. Did you tell Meera about Charles' being gay?"

Paulo took a step back. This hadn't even occurred to Charles. He had been so fixated on him selling the story.

"So what if I did?" Paulo replied. "He's a fucking fraud. You're the brave one. She was banging on about what a good signing, he'd been totally open with the world blah blah."

"And you set her straight?" Charles snarled.

Paulo glanced at him. "An unfortunate choice of words. I simply told her that you're still a liar. Always have been and always will be. My father said I should never trust a drunk. Deceit is in their veins."

Charles had reached his limit. He launched off the sofa and grabbed hold of Paulo, who let out a yelp. "You nasty little bastard," he roared. He pushed Paulo up against the wall and raised his fist. God, he wanted to smash it into that smug little face so badly. Luckily for Paulo, Luis grabbed hold of Charles' arm before he made contact.

"Saved again," Charles said, his face inches away from Paulo's. "One day, you won't be so lucky, Paulo. The way you carry on, someone will do the right thing and grind you to a pulp." He shoved Paulo away and walked over to the door.

"Charles, wait," Luis said.

Charles looked at the pair of them. His heart went out to Luis who had practically turned green, but he had to protect himself. "I'm sorry, Luis," he replied. "I don't need this."

"I bet you need a vodka though," Paulo muttered.

"Out," Luis roared.

This time Paulo did look rattled. "What?"

"You heard me," Luis replied. "I want you out of here."

"But—"

"Shall I just throw you out?" Charles growled. "It honestly would be my pleasure."

Pouting, Paulo stalked past Charles toward the door. "I wouldn't want you to exert yourself. At your age, it's probably not a good idea."

"Run along." Charles flashed him a sickly-sweet smile.

Paulo slammed the door behind him, and Charles exhaled loudly.

Luis seemed as though he were about to burst into tears. Charles dashed across the room and took him in his arms. This did trigger sobs. Stroking his back, Charles gave him the silence to get them out.

"I'm sorry," Luis said, eventually. "I had no idea he would do such a thing."

Charles couldn't decide if this were entirely true. How could Luis be ignorant that Paulo had a vicious side? Even so, he didn't want to argue. That would be playing right into Paulo's hands. "When money becomes involved, people lose their minds," he said, instead.

Luis slumped down on the couch. Charles sat opposite him. It reminded him of their showdown in the suite in Monaco.

"We always seem to be having drama," Luis replied. "Will we ever find steady ground?"

It touched Charles that Luis wanted this. Deep down, he wanted it too. More than anything. "I'd like to try," he said, truthfully.

Luis met his gaze. "Me too. I can't not have Paulo in my life. He's been my friend forever. I couldn't..."

Charles came forward and crouched between Luis' legs. He took hold of his hands and kissed them. "No one is asking you to," he said. "Although a bit of distance for the time being might be nice."

Luis stroked his hair. Charles felt so connected to him now that he yearned for him to give them the chance they needed.

"Agreed," he said. One word that made Charles' heart dance. "I'll send him home for the rest of the season. Don't worry, you won't get any trouble out of him again. I'll make it clear, if anything happens that I have the slightest inkling came from his hand, we will be finished."

Relief washed over Charles. He could match Paulo, but he hated wasting his energy on such shit. All he wanted to do now was to race and focus on developing whatever he had with Luis.

"I hope we don't get bored though." Luis sighed, a smile creeping over his face. "We seem to thrive on adrenaline."

Charles ran his hands up Luis' thighs. "I can find you some thrills. Don't worry about that."

"Now you're talking."

～

Two hours later and they were snuggled in bed. The blinds were shutting out the world and once again, they had created a bubble.

"Fuck, you're sexy," Charles said.

"If we keep this up, we could have had sex on every continent," Luis replied. "Imagine being able to say that."

"Except Antarctica," Charles replied. "That's a continent, right?"

Luis shrugged. "I'm hopeless at geography. Paulo has to tell me where we are a lot of the time."

Bloody Paulo. Charles tensed whenever he thought about that lizard. Luis must have noticed, as he sat up.

"Paulo has been like a brother to me," he said. "I can't lose him."

Paulo was always on the edge of the bubble with a great big needle, ready to make it pop.

"I understand," Charles conceded. "Keep him away from me for a long while though, eh?"

"Yes, that seems fair," Luis said. "You don't have to with Will. I don't blame him for what he did."

Sometimes the goodness in Luis that Charles had found so attractive became really fucking annoying. "There you go," Charles said. "Outdoing me. Now I look like the piece of shit."

Luis pinched him on the shoulder. "I think Paulo drew more blood. Don't be so sensitive."

At least Luis saw Paulo objectively for once. That wasn't a bad thing. "What hold does he have over you anyway?" Charles asked. "You put up with a lot from him."

Settling on the pillows, Luis faced Charles.

"When I started out, my parents had no money," he began.

"They had so many people in their ears telling them I should do this, I could be that. They desperately wanted to give me every chance. They sold everything and still it wasn't enough."

Driving fast cars could be an expensive hobby without rich sponsors. Charles realised how lucky he had been with his parents and chances. Money had never been a problem in the Worthington household. "And?" he prompted.

"Paulo's family were friends," Luis explained. "Paulo's father owns a factory in Rio. He sold it and put everything into me. It was the gamble of his life."

He had to respect a ballsy move like that, even by Charles' standards. No wonder Luis felt a debt to them. It didn't mean he had to give over his whole life though.

"He hasn't done badly out of it," Charles said.

"That's true," Luis agreed. "Even so, I will always owe them."

Frowning, Charles wanted to shake Luis. "That's bollocks. You've paid them back a hundred times over, I'm sure," he said. "You're an adult now."

Luis flushed. "You're right," he said. "Like I said, I will speak to Paulo tomorrow and suggest he goes home for the season."

Charles relaxed on the pillows. "That would be fucking amazing." He jumped as Luis flicked his nipple.

"He's still a friend," Luis reminded him.

"Blah, blah. Less talking." Charles grabbed hold of Luis and gently rolled him onto his back. "You're going to be way too busy for his games." He nuzzled Luis' neck. "And you know what? If we're going to fuck globally, we'd better get some practice in..."

CHAPTER NINETEEN

Sweat pumped from him as they walked onto the Crescent.

"He sounds like a grade-A shit," Alexander said.

"You're not wrong," Charles replied. "Unlucky for me, Luis thinks he's his best friend and I'm not getting in between them."

Alexander leant against the railings to the private gardens.

"It sounds to me that you did the right thing," he mused. "If Luis packs him off like you did with Will, the two of you might have a chance at properly getting to know each other. If that's what you want, of course."

The smile that followed these words was loaded.

"I do want that," Charles admitted. "More than I'm strictly comfortable with."

"Blimey," Alexander said, swigging from his bottle. "It's Mrs Wimpole I feel sorry for."

Charles frowned. "Mrs Wimpole?"

"Yes," Alexander grinned. "Imagine hell freezing over and she didn't get prior warning."

"You're a funny guy," Charles replied.

He took in the trees in the gardens. They were exploding with blossom, and the sight reminded him of his parents' house in the Cotswolds. Their estate would be incredible now. He wondered what Luis would think of them.

Steady on, Worthington. You're getting ahead of yourself again.

"I think there might be change on the horizon," he continued. "I've never felt like this before. It's terrifying."

Alexander considered him for a second. "I'm no expert on relationships," he began, "as the gutter press will delightfully inform you. Luis seems like a decent chap from what I've seen. I think you should go for it. Fuck it, what's the worst that can happen?"

Charles shrugged. Alexander reminded him a bit of Luis, in the fact that he lived his life with unashamed honesty. As a minor royal, that hadn't gone down well in all areas. Alexander had thumbed his nose at them and struck out on his own.

"I don't know," he replied. "The press getting hold of it, me and Luis break up spectacularly and I lose my job? That's not taking into account the bloody advertising contracts. I think Hilary has ad campaigns planned with them for the next five hundred years."

"You said change is coming," Alexander said. "You can't always control what form it takes."

The spring wind rustled through the trees, making Charles shiver

"Perhaps you're right," he replied. "Come on, we'd better get indoors. Mrs Wimpole is probably in one of the bushes right now."

"There's no need," Alexander replied drily. "She has them all bugged."

They walked up to their respective houses.

"Charles," Alexander said.

"What's up?"

"Be fearless. You never know where you land until you jump. Not really."

"Roger that."

Charles saluted and went up his own steps. Once inside, he thought about Alexander's words. When he had been in rehab, they had taught him to take control of his own life again. It had been the only thing that had got him through the last few months.

Can I give a little of it away now?

Glancing at the clock, he realised Luis would be here in fifteen minutes. They were spending the day together and Charles had plans. He ran up the stairs, throwing his clothes into the laundry basket before the warm jets of the shower did their usual trick of washing his cares away.

Wrapped in a towel, he took extra time getting those blond lucks into the perfect formation. Catching his own eye in the mirror, he made a silly face. "We will fucking jump," he said. Knowing his usual indecision about what to wear when it came to Luis, he had picked his outfit out the night before, a pair of ink blue chinos and a salmon shirt.

Luis would be expecting a day in bed. That would come in time. The doorbell rang and he bounded down the stairs. There he stood. Luis Salvatore. Strong, dependable and his.

"Hello, handsome," Charles said, knowing that special grin that only appeared when Luis was around was beaming out of him.

"Hello, yourself," Luis replied. "Aren't you going to let me in?"

Charles shook his head. "Nope. We're going out."

Grabbing his coat from the stand, he made his way out of the house.

"Wait," Luis said. "I want a kiss first."

Instinctively, Charles bent forward, but Luis stepped back. "Don't be crazy," he said. "Inside."

It felt like a rejection, even though he knew very well it

wasn't. Grumbling, he backed up into the hall and Luis kicked the door shut with his heel.

"Don't be grumpy," Luis chided.

Their lips met. The usual fire that Charles found so addictive swept around his body. Even underneath Luis' bulky woollen coat, Charles felt that hard body and craved it. Opening his mouth to Luis, he allowed his tongue inside. The kiss became more urgent, and Charles ran his hands through Luis' hair. They gasped for breath before kissing again. Charles pressed his body against Luis', revelling in the solid muscles that Charles loved to have around him as he slept. God, Luis could make him hard at fifty paces.

Charles pulled away. "We're going out, Mr Salvatore. I know what you're doing."

Luis rested his chin on Charles' shoulder. "Do we have to?"

Squirming out of his clutches, Charles beamed. "Yes, we bloody do. I've actually been romantic for once in my life. Don't fuck this up."

"Well, I suppose that is quite intriguing," Luis said. "Okay, although I will warn you. If it doesn't involve us naked together at some point, you're officially in the doghouse."

Charles reached down and cupped Luis' groin. He was reassured that underneath his jeans, Luis was hard as a rod. He squeezed. "He will be released. Have no fear."

Luis groaned. "That isn't fair."

"Go," Charles chuckled.

Complaining bitterly, Luis went outside. Charles locked the door and bounded down the steps.

"Someone is in a good mood today."

He might have known. "Hello, Mrs Wimpole. How are you today? And the Professor too?"

Mrs Wimpole and her friend, affectionately known as the Professor, were strolling up the Crescent, no doubt checking all was well in their little kingdom...or perhaps Alexander had been right. Charles wouldn't put it past the old dear to have surveillance equipment everywhere. She had the money, after all.

"All fine, young man," the Professor replied.

"And who is your handsome friend?" Mrs Wimpole enquired.

The Professor looked aghast. "That's Luis Salvatore," he stage-whispered.

She frowned. "I've heard the name. Are you another driver?"

"Yes, I am," Luis said with his trademark smile.

"A terribly noisy business," she replied. "I tried to watch when Charles first moved here. I'm more of a tennis fan. We all still support Charles though. Who wouldn't with that face?"

Charles wanted the ground to swallow him up.

"Very wise," Luis replied. "On both counts."

Mrs Wimpole raised an eyebrow and gave a very obvious nod to Charles. "We'll leave you be. Have a wonderful day."

Once they'd got into the safety of Charles' car, he noticed Luis had a big grin on his face. "Don't start," he said.

"That face though," Luis replied. "Who could resist it?"

Charles pouted. "Not you, evidently."

They spent the journey chattering about race gossip and proposed changes to their cars, and the names of Will and Paulo did not come up once. It felt as though they were both being very careful with each other. Charles appreciated that. The future was uncertain and deep down the terror kept trying to take a hold.

Even so, Charles felt happier than he had in ages. When it was just the two of them, everything became so effortless. Now a lot of their problems had been shoved onto the back burner, he hoped desperately they were at the beginning of something special. If it wasn't, he was going to be a prize idiot when they reached their destination.

They made their way into Mayfair.

"At least I know it won't be burger on plastic seats again," Luis said, staring out of the window at the expensive boutiques and perfect little wine bars.

They were nearly there, and Charles took a deep breath as they turned the corner. He drew up outside and let the engine die.

"Claridge's?" Luis asked.

"I booked us afternoon tea," Charles replied. "I wanted to be the decent man to bring you here."

Tears welled in Luis' eyes, and he looked down. Instantly Charles realised he'd misjudged this and muscled in on a dream of Luis'.

"I'm sorry," he continued, babbling in the way he did when nerves got the better of him. "I thought it would be a nice gesture. Shit, I never even thought it wasn't my thing to get involved in. Forget I did anything. We can do something else."

He went to start the car again, but Luis' hand stayed him.

"I'm not upset because of that, you idiot," he said. "In fact, I'm not upset at all. This is such a lovely thing to do, and I would absolutely love for you to be the decent man to share this with."

Charles reddened. "I want to kiss your face off right now," he said.

"Outside Claridge's would not be the right place," Luis replied. "For the record, I want to kiss yours off too."

The frustration made Charles want to throw caution to the wind. The man he was rapidly falling for sat inches from him, but the streets were way too busy to do anything about it. Every tourist with a camera phone could be a potential paparazzi these days.

They got out of the car, Charles handed the keys to the valet, and they walked through the doors into one of the most famous hotels in the city.

Charles had stayed there many times over the years when he wanted a change or if attending a function there. Once he'd began earning the big bucks, London had been at his disposal. Boy, had he made the most of it.

The cream room that housed the great British tradition of afternoon tea was a hive of activity. The clink of the striped china and hushed conversation of people enjoying the ultimate in luxury dipped when Charles and Luis walked in.

A nervous waiter led them to a table in the corner. It was too much to expect that they wouldn't be gawped at. What he wouldn't give for one of those glasses of champagne that were being served all over the room.

The waiter rubbed his hands together. "Before we begin, would you like to upgrade to our champagne offering?" he asked.

Luis shook his head. "Just the tea will suffice, thank you."

Charles pitied the poor waiter when he realised what he had said.

"Oh yes, of course." He dashed off.

"Poor thing." Charles laughed. "I thought for a second someone might not know about me."

"You did do it in the full glare of the papers," Luis replied. "It will take a bit of time."

Even though they were in a very exclusive place, Charles could see eyes being trained on him. Where eyes went, camera phones followed. "We'll probably be in the papers tomorrow," he said. "Someone in this room will make a bit off us."

Luis glanced around. "Oh, good luck to them," he said. "You can say I lost a bet about something. I'm sure we can maintain your alpha image somehow."

Charles had been about to say something when the waiter returned with pots of tea for them. He glanced nervously at them as he placed them on the table.

"This looks wonderful," Charles said.

The young lad beamed. "I'm not supposed to let on, but I think you're brilliant," he said to Charles.

"Thank you," Charles replied.

"Oh, and you, Mr Salvatore. Of course."

Luis grinned. "Of course."

The young lad left them blushing harder than he had the first time.

"It's not his day today," Charles chuckled. "I'll tip him well."

Luis raised his cup. "To making young boys blush."

They clinked. Charles had relaxed now. Luis did that to him. People were still nosing at them. Once he'd done the deal with the devil and got fame, he found to his shock that it was very difficult to reverse it.

"That evens us up a bit," Charles said. "Those kids at the PR event were convinced I'd sneaked into that burger joint. It was all I could do to convince them I was allowed even a packet of fries."

Luis didn't even attempt to hide his amusement. "They were a tough crowd," he agreed. "I love it though. Let kids be kids."

Charles nodded. He loved it when Luis' face lit up. Silently, he vowed to make that happen as much as possible from now on.

"I used to come here with my granny," Charles said. "We weren't allowed to speak."

"Doesn't sound like much fun," Luis replied.

His granny wasn't all that interested in fun. She thrived on decorum and routine. She had died when he was in his teens. He hadn't been that upset. "No," Charles said. "It wasn't. She didn't subscribe to kids being kids, that's for sure."

The blushing waiter returned with two big cake stands laden with sandwiches, delicate treats and scones.

"The car will never set off at this rate," Luis groaned, rubbing his still six-packed belly.

"Oh, we can arrange for you to have a doggy bag," the waiter replied.

"Thank goodness for that," Luis said.

"I hope you enjoy it."

"Thank you."

Charles flashed him his winning smile and sent him away, crimson.

"I think he fancies you," Luis whispered.

"He's only human," Charles replied.

Luis grimaced. "You won't find anything as delicious on there as you find yourself."

Leaning forward, Charles let his hand brush over Luis'. "And you don't?"

"I didn't say that."

"Good, because you haven't found out what part two of my surprise is yet."

CHAPTER TWENTY

Luis lay spreadeagled on the bed, his hard muscles glowing in the early evening sun which broke through the gap in the heavy drapes. Charles ran his hands over Luis' body. He wanted to touch every part. Discover it all over again.

"God, your touch drives me crazy," Luis whispered.

Taking this as further encouragement, Charles homed in on the areas he had discovered made Luis twitch all the more. He stroked the inside of his thigh, making him squirm, then let his fingers lightly dance over his hip bones and up to his nipples. Other than the obvious, that was the area that drove Luis the wildest.

He pinched then leant down, licking his left nipple before moving over to the right. As he came up and their eyes met, he thought his heart might burst. Luis stared back at him. Fighting a pathetic sob, Charles kissed Luis' chest. It had only been weeks but something about this man had burrowed deep inside him

"What is it?" Luis asked.

"Nothing," Charles replied, softly. "I just like being with you."

Luis wrapped his arm around Charles' shoulder, pulling him in for a kiss. "I like being with you too. But…"

Charles moved to see Luis properly. "But what?"

"We're taking a hell of a risk, being here."

The second part of Charles' surprise had been the keys to a suite upstairs in Claridge's. They'd polished off most of the afternoon tea. The rest sat in two little boxes on the coffee table of the lounge.

Rolling onto his back, Charles cursed their lack of privacy. "That's why I went with two bedrooms," he said. "Just in case anyone blabs. We can say we have a function tonight. Surely, they won't be checking that closely."

He'd lost his erection and Luis clearly noticed. "I'm sorry," he said, kissing his earlobes. "I've ruined the moment."

Suddenly, Charles felt claustrophobic. He got up off the bed and walked over to the window. It opened to a small balcony that had a spectacular view over the rooftops of Mayfair.

The sun had set, and the early spring chill made people pick up the pace to wherever they were headed. They could be on dates where they would kiss freely, perhaps hold hands if things were going that well. Charles envied them their freedoms.

"Charles," Luis said. "Talk to me."

A worried Luis sat upright in bed. At that moment, Charles realised he wanted to see that every night. He wanted to wake up with this man every morning.

"I'm having a moment," Charles said.

He sat down in a chair in the corner of the room. Luis scooted to the end of the bed, reaching out for him, but Charles held his hands up. "Can we just talk for a second?"

Nodding, Luis sat cross-legged on the bed. Of course, his posture would be absolutely perfect.

"Go on," Luis said, reassuringly. "You can say anything to me. Surely you know that now."

The anxiety made his chest tight. Charles hated doing this

shit. He'd been forced to speak about his feeling so many times at rehab. It never got any easier. Weirdly, it made him want to do it more. Yet the actual act still felt like he was having something removed. Without anaesthetic.

"Are we a thing?" he blurted out.

Then he realised how fucking stupid it sounded. Would he offer to carry Luis' bags home after P.E. next?

"A thing?" Luis asked, a grin spreading on his face. "Depends on what a thing is."

"Don't make this any harder than it has to be," Charles grumbled. "You know what I mean."

He would rather stick pins in his eyes at that moment than have such an awkward conversation. It appeared that Luis was rather enjoying himself, which annoyed him even further.

"A thing suggests we're seeing each other," Luis continued. "Yes, I think this can safely be called a thing."

"I'm going to slap your arse in a minute," Charles muttered.

"I wish you would," Luis replied. "I don't take kindly to soft ons." He nodded at Charles' groin which Charles covered with a cushion.

"If you could keep my cock out of it for a minute," he said. "If we're a thing, then we're doing this. I'm not fucking around in the shadows."

Luis mouth dropped open. "Do you realise what you are saying?"

Charles nodded. He had thought about it until he was sick of thinking. Being open and honest about their relationship to the world meant the pressure of hiding dissolved. Of course, other strains would replace it. If they faced them as a unit, though, they had a better chance of surviving.

"Yeah, I do," he replied. "I'm done with all this pretending. Today taught me that I don't give a fuck what people think, I want to sit and have afternoon tea with you. If I choose to hold your hand, I don't want to be afraid to show the world that I'm falling in love with you."

As soon as the last few words tumbled out of his mouth, he realised he might have gone too far.

Luis stared at him, stunned. "Do you mean that?"

He had set off down this road of honesty. He might as well see where it led. "Yeah. I really fucking do. I really, really mean it."

Luis moved forward. "Wait, am I allowed to touch you yet?"

Grinning, Charles opened his arms. Luis threw the cushion to one side and straddled him. Charles kissed him as though it were their last kiss. He wanted every part of their bodies connected. He hadn't meant to just come out with it like that but now he'd said it, he relished the weight lifting from his shoulders.

Luis stroked Charles' hair. "For the record, I'm falling in love with you too."

The relief was huge. If Luis had suggested they take it slow, he would have literally died of embarrassment. Deep down, Charles had known he wouldn't. There weren't many things he was sure of in the world and most of them had four wheels. However, Charles knew with absolutely certainty that Luis remained along for the ride, the same as he did.

He reached across for his mobile phone and connected a call. Luis shifted and kissed his cheek.

"Hello?" The unmistakable voice of Hilary Milligan rang out of the phone speaker.

"Hill? It's your darling dashing driver."

"Why am I suddenly nervous? What do you want?"

He winked at Luis. "What would the impact be if I were to come out?"

There was silence on the other end of the line.

"Hilary?"

"Are you fucking crazy?"

"Do you think you could handle the fallout?"

"What are you planning? Charles? I mean it. You'd better tell me. In fact, where are you? Wherever it is, I'm coming over."

Charles laughed. "I think you'd better get some press releases ready."

"Charles. Honestly, you're giving me palpitations. What are you going to do?"

He had never heard her so shrill in his life. "I'm done with pretending," he said, eventually. "Come over to the house in the morning. I think we might need you."

"Oh Jesus, you said we. You're with Luis Salvatore, aren't you?"

"Hi, Hilary," Luis chimed in.

"This is the worst phone call of my life. We have campaigns with major brands. Okay, right. Let me think," she blabbered. "Have you spoken to others? Meera? Anyone?"

Charles winked at Luis. "Only you, my sweet. Only you. Anyway, we've got to go. Speak to you tomorrow."

"Charles—"

He terminated the call.

Luis stared into his eyes. "What are you going to do? Now we're a thing, can you stop this man-of-mystery shit. It's not cool."

"Do you know Bill Ward?" Charles asked, running his finger up Luis' arm.

Luis frowned. "The paparazzi man? He's a total twat."

"That's what I thought," Charles said. "Then he killed a ton of stories about me. He holds a lot of sway with the others, and he told them to leave off. Obviously, some didn't, but things could have been a lot worse for me."

"Why would he do that?"

"Turns out, he's a reformed alcoholic himself."

"Wow," Luis said. "People surprise you all the time, don't they?"

Charles nodded. "Like I did for you?"

Kissing his nose, Luis grinned. "Absolutely. Anyway, what has Bill Ward got to do with anything?"

"I thought we could give him an exclusive," Charles said. "Pay him back for a good turn." Charles' heart hammered inside his ribcage. Being in love did not feel healthy. He knew he would be coming across as incredibly needy right now, but he refused to put the brakes on.

"Are you sure?" Luis asked. "Once it's done, it can't be undone."

"If you're with me," Charles said, "then I don't care."

Luis ran his hands through Charles' hair. "I'm with you."

The plan had been set. Charles terminated the call and went into the bedroom. He found a naked Luis watching him intently. "You look spectacular," he said, leaning against the doorframe.

"What did he say?"

"He said he'd be here in fifteen," Charles said. "This is the moment he's waited for all his bloody life."

Luis sat up. "Did you tell him it was with me?"

"No," Charles replied, flopping down on the bed. "I thought I'd let that be a surprise. I just said my new and permanent lover."

Luis kissed him. "I like the sound of that. Permanent lover."

Charles rolled him onto his back and returned his kiss. "What should I call you?" he said. "I fear we'll be made to define ourselves tomorrow."

Running his hands down Charles' body and sending tingles up his spine, Luis seemed lost in thought for a second.

"I think partners says it," he decided. "You're too old to be my boyfriend."

"Hey," Charles said.

Luis giggled and kissed his neck. "Sorry, Daddy."

Charles dug him in the ribs, making him laugh out loud. "You can quit that shit."

"So, fifteen minutes," Luis said. "What to do with ourselves...?"

Charles silenced him with another kiss. This time their tongues met, and the passion ignited. The nerves at what they were about to do were intense and he needed that closeness with Luis. His cock ached for Luis. His hard on had returned with a vengeance.

Reaching down, Luis took hold of him. He gasped. Luis' touch made him feel alive. They broke the kiss, and he buried his face in Luis' neck, smelling the citrus aroma of his cologne. Then something underneath, musky, his real scent.

Charles licked his neck, making Luis groan.

They shifted so Charles lay with Luis straddled across him. Luis stared deep into his eyes. Charles returned the stare. With anyone else, he would have looked away, embarrassed. Now he wanted to let Luis see deep within him. Luis leant down and kissed him tenderly. It was the kind of kiss that made Charles' whole body respond. He felt so close and warm, a tear escaped his eye.

Luis worked his way down Charles' body, paying attention to every part of him. When he got to Charles' cock, he let his breath fall on it. The heat from him made Charles' erection strain. Then he took him all in his mouth. Charles grabbed the sheets, twisting them in his fist as Luis held him there.

"Oh, fuck, Luis—"

He sucked him hard now. The whole mood had changed from sensual to passion, as though Luis couldn't contain himself anymore. Coming up for air, Charles sat back. They clashed in the middle. Their strong arms grappled with each other and they kissed furiously, letting their tongues dance together.

With his other hand, he reached down and took hold of Luis' hard cock. Luis did the same and they jacked each other. Never breaking the kiss, Charles focused on Luis' pleasure.

Luis started to moan. Charles also felt close. He gripped Luis' shoulder.

Then his body was overwhelmed with pleasure as the orgasm ripped through him. His heart pounding, the world stopped mattering for that split second. Then he came crashing back to earth. He was still kissing Luis.

The kiss slowed and eventually they broke.

"Fucking hell," Luis panted.

"Indeed."

He went through to the ensuite and cleaned himself with a towel. Luis followed him. Once they'd finished, Luis ran his hands over Charles' chest. "You're something, Charles Worthington."

"Thank you, Luis Salvatore. You're not so bad yourself."

"Ready?"

Charles nodded. "Ready?"

They threw on the impossibly white and ridiculously fluffy bathrobes and made their way out onto the balcony. Having no idea where Bill would be hiding, they turned this way and that to make sure he would get their faces.

Suddenly, Charles caught the unmistakable sound of a camera shutter going off in the distance. "Come here," he said.

He snaked his arm around Luis' waist and drew him close. Luis looked up and the reassurance that Charles found in his eyes was something he'd never come close to before.

They kissed. It was probably the most important kiss in Charles' life. As the camera clicked away, Charles lost himself in the moment.

This would change everything.

CHAPTER TWENTY-ONE

Photographers crowded the entrance to Queens Crescent as Charles drove down the main street. He considered changing his plans, not going home but instead just carrying on and getting a flight somewhere. But he wouldn't get far without a passport, which was in a safe inside his house.

He pulled over to the opposite side of the road. He hadn't even thought that the scrum of photographers would reach Queens Crescent. "Oh fuck," he lamented. "Mrs Wimpole will have us killed."

"I wouldn't be so sure," Luis replied, pointing.

There stood little Mrs Wimpole, backed up by the portly Professor. She was gesticulating wildly at the photographers who, to their credit, were terrified. Charles wound his window down.

"Move over there," Mrs Wimpole ordered. "This is a private road."

Parkin, her ever-present Yorkshire terrier, nipped at the heels of the offending photographer who had stepped foot in her kingdom.

The Professor was armed with an umbrella and jabbed

menacingly at another photographer who was trying to get a shot of Charles' house. "You get back, you vermin," he roared. "What kind of a living is this? Why don't you do something you can be proud of?"

His opponent was a little lighter on his feet than Mrs Wimpole's adversary and he dodged the Professor's feints. Once he'd got his shot, he backed off, laughing.

"And don't come back," the Professor shouted after him.

"Are you ready?" Charles asked. "We should probably get involved before we have to take a photographer to A&E."

"We're all over social media," Luis answered him. "What's one more photo?"

The first photographer recognised the car and made a beeline for them. The rest quickly cottoned on and it became a full-blown rugby scrum as Charles tried to turn off the main road. To his amazement, Mrs Wimpole, complete with walking stick, beat a path on one side. The Professor, now quite adept, cleared the other. Charles wound his window down.

"Mrs Wimpole," he said. "Are you all right?"

"I am perfectly all right," she assured him, the colour in her cheeks underlining that yes, she was. "I am reminding these gentlemen that Queens Crescent is a private road and they can't put so much as the toes of one foot in it." She roared the last few words in the press' direction. "Now, in you go."

Charles beamed at her. "I bloody love you, Mrs W."

She raised an eyebrow slightly. "Never mind all that," she ordered. "Just you get inside."

He managed to get his car into the little road with no inci-dent. The shutters went off all the more as he and Luis got out of the vehicle, the photographers shouting and jostling to get the shot. Charles refused to reward them, and he and Luis walked apart into the house.

When they got in, Charles let out a sigh. "Good old Mrs Wimpole and the Prof, eh?"

"I wouldn't mess with her," Luis replied.

They walked through into the kitchen. It was weird that everything looked exactly the same. But since Charles had last stood in here, his whole life had taken a new direction.

"You okay?" Luis asked.

Charles wrapped his arms around him. "More than that. I think the phones are going to be going off today."

"Fuck them," Luis said.

"Agreed."

He kissed Luis. They had spent the whole night in each other's arms, but it never seemed enough. "You hungry?"

"Starving," he replied.

Claridge's hadn't been too happy at their little publicity stunt. The place had soon been recognised. Press and fans had swarmed the outside by the time they got up in the morning, and the manager had told them sternly that they liked to be informed if the hotel was to be used in that way.

They had thought it best not to stay for breakfast.

Charles busied himself getting the coffee on and toast made. They had eggs and bacon so he could most certainly rustle something up.

"Did you see that fan outside the hotel?" Luis asked.

"No," Charles replied. "I was too busy getting in the bloody car. What about them?"

"They had a sign saying *Love is love.*"

Charles stopped. "That's nice," he said. "I haven't dared check what the temperature is like with the fans. I'm lusted after by many women, you know."

Luis burst out laughing. "Am I going to be public enemy number one?"

"Oh, most certainly," Charles agreed. He cracked the eggs into a bowl and whisked. "What time is it?"

"Nearly nine," Luis replied. "Are we staying indoors today, do you think?"

"I think that's probably wise. Unless you fancied a trip to Oxford Street or maybe a football match?"

Luis considered, his head on one side. "Oh, I think we'll find plenty to do here."

A sudden loud banging on the door made them start. Had people stopped ringing bells these days?

"What the fuck?" Luis exclaimed. "Has one of them got past Mrs Wimpole?"

Charles put the bowl down. "No, it's worse than that. There's only one person in the world who doesn't use my bell."

He strode down the hallway and opened the door. Hilary stood on the step. Her hair was all over the place and her eyebags had bags. The poor thing clearly hadn't had any sleep since his phone call.

"Well, you've made quite the splash, haven't you?" She didn't wait for a reply and barged in the house.

"We're in the kitchen," Charles said as he followed her through.

She plonked her bag down on the table and sat next to Luis. "Coffee, please."

Charles shot Luis a glance as he poured three cups. Hilary would have wanted to micromanage this and he braced himself for the inevitable. "Hil—"

She held her hand up. "Wait. I've got something to say first. Sit down."

Charles bristled at being told what to do in his own kitchen. Even so, he gingerly sat down next to Luis and reached for his hand. "Go on then," he said.

"Firstly, I'm very happy for you, Charles."

His mouth dropped.

"Oh, don't look like that," Hilary continued. "You know you're my favourite. You always have been. I do wish you'd given me some bloody notice. I could have got you an exclusive."

"That's the point though," Charles said. "I didn't want to do it that way. I'm not being accused of profiting from it."

Hilary waved him away. "Don't talk crap. Everyone profits from shit like this. It's a bit bloody late now though. Bill Ward thinks he's won the frigging lottery."

Charles didn't care. He just wanted to lock the door and never let anyone else in the house again. He also knew the game and that a grainy paparazzi photo wouldn't be the end of this.

"What can you do?"

A smile crept over Hilary's face. "You can always rely on me. I've been up all bloody night, but I've got you a sit-down web link interview with Anderson Cooper later. You gave me enough notice for that anyway. *Architectural Digest* are interested in doing an at-home video thing. I'm waiting to hear from *Attitude, Gay Times*, and *The Advocate*."

Charles loved her more at that moment than he had over all the years they'd been together. "Fucking hell, Hill," he said. "You've been busy."

"This might not be my usual market. Never let it be said I can't pivot," Hilary replied. "I came round this morning to warn you. If you step one foot out of this house until I've got these in the bag, I will personally chop your bollocks off. Both of you."

Luis grinned. "I'm not your client."

"You are now," she fired back. "I've not protected this layabout for ten years for nothing. This is the first time I've brokered anything remotely positive for you."

"Hang on a minute..." Charles interjected.

"When? Name one positive story in ten years, Charles."

He thought about it but his mind drew a blank. Surely he had done something good in the last decade.

"I hosted that group of women in Vegas for the *Celebrity Slave Auction* show."

Hilary raised an eyebrow. "How selfless of you."

"I will speak to my agent," Luis said with a perplexed frown

"Already done," Hilary replied. "We've come up with a deal. I'm doing UK/US press and they're covering the rest. Seems fair when I have the contacts. Nihal Varma will be fucking livid and if Meera thinks she's poaching this for her campaigns—"

"I think Meera has a stake," Luis replied.

"Do you want the money to go to South Tel or your foundation?" Hilary asked.

Luis took a sip of his coffee. "You have a deal."

"Fine," Hilary continued. "South Tel can have you at the next race. The initial furore will be over then. Right, I'm going to the office. Heed my words though, you don't even go to the shop for a pint of milk. Is that understood?"

"Loud and clear," Charles said. "And thank you."

Hilary got up and flung her bag over her shoulder. "I think you're very brave, Charles Worthington," she said, planting a kiss firmly on his cheek. "I'll get back to you boys." Not waiting for a reply, she swept out of the house, banging the door behind her.

"With Mrs Wimpole and Hilary on our side, we can rule the world." Luis laughed.

Charles took hold of his hand. "It sounds like we're going to be a hot couple." He kissed Luis.

Luis kissed him back. "I can handle that," Luis replied.

"Me too."

Charles kissed him again, to prove it.

They were lying top to tail on the couch, naked and under the soft throw Charles had bought in Morocco. Just feeling the heat from Luis comforted him.

Luis was busy checking out social media on his phone.

Charles watched him, the screen lighting his face up in the dusk light.

"I can tell you're staring," Luis said, not looking up.

Charles grinned. "I'm allowed, aren't I?"

Luis met his gaze. "I guess so, weirdo."

Throwing his phone down, Luis stretched. Charles couldn't take his eyes from the muscles flexing under his skin as the throw fell down. "Yum."

"We haven't moved for two hours. House arrest is fun."

Running his foot against Luis' body, Charles felt so happy right now. "What's the story on the socials?" he asked. "Are they out to tar and feather us?"

Shrugging, Luis took hold of Charles' foot and massaged it. Charles sank onto the cushions. Luis had the touch.

"Most people are positive," Luis replied. "There are some wankers on there, but isn't there always?"

Charles nodded. He'd long since stopped checking his social media. He let Jennifer in Hilary's office deal with all that now. She sent him some of the decent stuff and shielded him from most of the trolls.

"Fancy a swim?" Charles asked.

Luis shook his head. "I just want to stay here," he replied, putting more pressure on Charles' foot. "You have some tension that needs me."

"My tension needs your attention?"

Luis chuckled. "Don't give up the day job."

Groaning, Charles rubbed his eyes. "The day job? Meera has been very silent."

That they hadn't heard a thing from her unnerved them both. Charles glanced at his phone.

"Get it done," Luis said. "Give her a call."

"I like the way I'm the one that has to ring. We're both equals."

"I'm here, aren't I?" Luis said. "If it gets too much, just grab hold of me. Try not to get us both sacked though. That's all I ask."

Charles stuck his tongue out. But he still made the call. She answered in one ring.

"About fucking time," she blurted out. "Are you all right?"

Her concern touched him. "We're fine," he replied. "Do we still have jobs?"

Luis rolled his eyes. "*Subtle,*" he mouthed at Charles.

"Of course you do. Now I understand where all that rivalry came from. You little boys and your blue balls. I should have known."

Trust Meera to put her own spin on things. Clearly, she wasn't getting caught up in their love story. Charles wouldn't have it any other way.

"I presume lover boy is with you," Meera continued.

"He is."

"Fine, I'll get this off my chest once then," she replied. "If you pull a stunt like that again without consulting me, I will personally remove all of your genitals and sell them on eBay for charity."

Luis made a face.

"Now to today's business that's royally fucked up my Sunday with my family," she said. "Let's weather the storm and fuck them up on the racetrack. Do I make myself clear?"

The relief hit him right in the chest like a ten-ton truck. He ran his hands through his hair and scrambled to focus on what she was saying. He had everything now. A wonderful man and a career.

He locked eyes with Luis and saw everything in there. Trust, hope, and love. It had taken him such a long time to get here, but now he'd arrived, Charles let the happiness envelop him entirely.

"Thank you, Meera," he said. "You have no idea what this means."

"I do," she replied. "It means a lot of hard work and results. I'm watching you both."

As usual for her, she terminated the call before he had a chance to get the final word. He threw the phone onto the coffee table.

"That was positive," Luis said.

"I know," Charles agreed. "What a bloody day this is turning out to be."

They shared a look that was loaded with more than passion, something stronger than that. Charles had never been in love, and he wondered if this was it. He would kill anyone who even tried to harm Luis. He also would be lost without him now.

Sounds like love to me.

"What are you thinking about?" Luis asked.

"You."

Luis blushed. "When you were straight, you were the biggest player in town. Now you're gay, you're very full on."

Charles beamed. "You make me full on."

Stopping the massage and caressing his foot, Luis sighed. "We're a team on and off the track now. This season is going to be fucking amazing."

"Carry on with that massage," Charles said. "I'll need those feet in tip-top shape to get to that number podium all those times."

Luis slapped his foot. "I think you'll find I was the last one up there."

"You know what?" Charles said. "I don't even care which of us it is. What have you done to me?"

Luis didn't laugh. He just stared at Charles. "I love you."

The most powerful three words in the business and they were his. Tears welled in Charles' eyes. "I love you too," he replied. "Truly I do."

Throwing the covers to one side, he scrambled up the sofa towards Luis.

His future.

~

Thank you for reading *Pole Position*.
If you liked it, I'd be grateful for a review on Goodreads or
Amazon.

To keep up to date with all my news, head to www. kristianparker.com to sign up to my monthly newsletter, or my Facebook Reader Group kristiansworld.

I'm back in May 2023 with the next book from this billionaire's row. *Reality Royal* sees minor royal, Alexander Fitzwilliam meet daytime soap star, Zac Caton. They are paired together on the hit reality TV series, Celebrity Blogger.

Keep reading for an exclusive extract from *Reality Royal*. Enjoy!

REALITY ROYAL

The hot studio lights beamed down on Alexander Fitzwilliam and a trickle of sweat crawled down his back. He wished he hadn't worn a suit in the middle of summer. With a damp palm, he smoothed back his blonde hair. The hair department had put a million products in it. Great, now he would have sticky and sweaty palms to meet his mystery partner.

The studio audience stared at him as one. Alexander put on his best smile, ignoring the churning in the pit of his stomach. This was going to be a week in his life running a blog with a celebrity partner. The show was ramping up the tension by having a glittery screen leaving the big reveal to the final moment.

"You seem a bit nervous there, Alexander." Amber Jade, prime time TV host and darling of the gossip columns, grinned at him.

"I just hope I have a wonderful partner," Alexander stammered. "Then we can give the people what they want."

The audience burst into applause.

"Let's bring him in," Amber shouted. "Your fate is in our hands."

Cheesy theme music blared out. Everyone except

Alexander could see who had entered the studio. It had to be someone decent because a good amount of people cheered wildly. A woman in the front row gave him a thumbs-up whilst nodding furiously. Judging by the skin-tight pink boob tube she had on, they could well have very different tastes, though.

"Okay, folks," Amber said to the audience. "Are we ready?"

The audience screamed wildly.

"Slide it back," Amber shouted, waving her hands at the audience.

They joined in the chant. When the noise reached fever pitch, the screen shakily rolled back. Alexander smoothed his suit jacket and turned to face his future.

Who would be on the other side? He didn't even care that much, yet found himself swept along with the excitement of the moment. Alexander prayed it wouldn't be one of the cast of the new reality television series, *Chip Shop Wars*. He had no desire to smell like vinegar and fried food for a week.

Jesus H Christ. It's only Zac Caton!

Facing one of the most handsome men on television, Alexander's knees almost gave way underneath him. Zac grinned at Alexander, his pearly white teeth dazzling. He was like a younger Stanley Tucci with barely there stubble, horn rimmed glasses and a bald head.

"Zac Caton, meet Alexander Fitzwilliam," Amber Jade shouted.

Zac, resplendent in a tight-fitting denim shirt and chinos, stepped forward and drew Alexander into a hug. His strong arms made Alexander almost yelp, if he hadn't remembered the mic attached to him. The inviting spicy smell of Zac made Alexander want to stay in those arms for a good hour if not more.

"Pleased to meet you," Zac said in the deep timbre that Alexander recognised instantly.

"And you," Alexander managed, regretfully allowing Zac to step away.

He caught Zac's eye who grinned and looked away. Before they could say anymore, Amber Jade pushed her way in between them. "This looks like a winning team," she declared. "Alexander, are you happy with your partner?"

"Oh, absolutely," Alexander said, regaining his composure. "Who doesn't love Hamish Beattie?"

A few members of the audience screamed wildly. As one of the longest-serving cast members in the daytime soap *Highland Fling*, Zac had a loyal fanbase. Usually, Alexander would crawl over hot coals rather than admit to watching it. In reality, he had tuned in once or twice when crippled by yet another hangover. Watching Zac deal with the problems of his fictional village was the perfect way to spend half an hour.

"And, Zac? How are you feeling?"

Zac appraised Alexander as though a farmer would a prize cow at the market. "A real member of the aristocracy?" he said. "Lucky me."

"Very minor," Alexander assured him.

"Soap and royalty," Amber Jade declared. "What a combination. We will see you next week to find out who will win this week's *Celebrity Blogger*. Zac, take your partner to the couches."

Alexander had barely looked at the handsome Zac since the screen had gone back. If he dared catch his eye again, he would be blushing like a spring bride on national television. Women all over the country had posters of Zac up, even though he had a very public coming out a few years ago. It didn't seem to matter.

"Shall we?" Zac asked with a grin.

"Absolutely."

To his joy, he felt Zac's hand in the small of his back. Alexander allowed himself to be guided to a bright green sofa where their opponents were waiting. The camera tracked them as the audience clapped wildly.

Derek and Dora Smedley scowled across at them. The couple in their sixties, famous for roller skating tricks back in the nineties, who had been paired with Wayne Schofield, an ex-Premiership footballer. Alexander found it slightly unfair that the Smedleys came as one.

The second partnership consisted of hot new rapper, Blade, and pop princess, Holly Hock. The atmosphere between them did not appear to be friendly. Then Alexander remembered they had had a fling on *Celebrity Carol Singing*. It clearly hadn't ended well.

Alexander settled on the couch. The television company were paying him a fortune for this appearance. He'd figured it would be a week's work and that would be that. Now that Zac's hand rested on his shoulder, he found himself genuinely looking forward to it, although he didn't expect to see that much of the handsome soap star. He glanced up and there was that impossibly bright smile. Zac winked at him.

"Zac and Alexander," Amber Jade shouted. Alexander wanted to remind her that she had a microphone in her hand. She had absolutely no need to holler every word on the autocue. "Who is going to spin the wheel of destiny? We know what that means don't we folks?"

The audience all cheered "Yes" as one. Then Amber Jade stared down the camera. "But for those at home who don't. The wheel of destiny will decide the vibe of our contestants blogs. Partnerships have been smashed to smithereens by the unforgiving wheel."

The audience screamed wildly as a sparkly wheel was brought out.

"I'm happy for you to do it," Zac said. Every time he stared at Alexander, his eyes seemed to bore into Alexander's soul. He found it quite disconcerting.

"Are you sure?"

Zac nodded. "I trust you."

"Famous last words," Alexander said as he allowed Amber Jade to lead him to the prop. Waiting a second to get the crowd on side, he gave it an almighty spin. Cue appropriate noises from the audience. It stopped on *New Experiences*.

Alexander glanced at Zac, who shrugged. "I love new experiences."

"Don't we all?" Alexander replied, forgetting where he was for a second.

The audience didn't miss that and all whooped. Zac went crimson and looked away. Thankfully he was laughing.

"I can see we're going to have to watch you two," Amber Jade bellowed.

As Amber Jade dragged Dora of rollerskating fame toward the wheel, Zac rested his hand on Alexander's shoulder again. It was an intimate act from someone he'd never met before, yet in a strange way, totally natural.

The wheel stopped on *Cooking*. The crowd cheered as Wayne scowled. Alexander hoped that meant they had a chance.

Holly was the final person up and she spun the wheel as fast as her false nails would allow. It stopped on *Interview*. She frowned at Blade, who couldn't have been more disinterested.

"There we have it, folks. These are our teams," Amber Jade boomed. "You know how it works. Every day, you post an article on the *Celebrity Blogger* Blog. Whoever has the most hits by next Saturday wins ten thousand pounds for the charity of their choice."

Once more the excitable crowd clapped wildly.

Amber Jade let them settle before grinning at a camera with a big red light on. "And that's all for part one. Don't forget to come back after the break to find out who won last week's competition."

Theme music boomed out around the studio. As soon as the

red light disappeared, makeup artists and hair stylists descended on Amber Jade.

"I think we have to go," Zac said.

He still had a strong English accent. However, after ten years in the Scottish Highlands, he had more than a trace of the scotch brogue.

Alexander followed him off the studio floor, giving the audience one last wave. "How obvious that they put the gays together," he said as they got into the green room.

The tiny little room was far too hot. Alexander loosened his collar a little. Their opponents were already huddling in corners.

"Do you want a drink?" Zac asked him.

"Sure," Alexander replied, trying to sound as cool as possible.

Stop trying so hard, Fitzwilliam. He will think you are weird.

He watched Zac go over to the table filled with supermarket booze and crisps. Alexander had lusted after Zac from his sofa for years. In person he was even more gorgeous. Zac Caton owned the fact that he had passed forty. He didn't try to compete with younger folk. Instead, he seemed perfectly comfortable in his own niche.

"Hot, eh?" Amber Jade said, breaking into his thoughts. He hadn't even heard her sidle up to him.

"Yes, it is a little warm in here," he replied.

Amber Jade gave him a knowing grin before sloping off to speak to the roller-skaters. On her way she said something to a cameraman, who looked over at Alexander.

Zac came back, balancing two bottles of beer. "The wine was pretty warm. I didn't think you'd be up for that," he said to Alexander. "I'm sure you have very high standards."

"Beer's fine." Alexander accepted the bottle. "Although when I backpacked around Vietnam, I got partial to warm wine. One learns survival techniques, I suppose."

He noticed the raised eyebrow from Zac. "What's the matter?" he asked. "Did you think I came here in a gilt carriage drawn by unicorns?"

"Of course not," Zac said, sinking down on the sofa. "I thought you'd prefer winged cherubs."

"Oh, you're funny," Alexander replied, drily. "How marvellous."

Zac grinned at him. "You'll be surprised by the extent of my talents."

"Hidden under a Scottish rock all these years? What do you think they'll have us doing? I hope it's not too humiliating."

A furore broke out at the other end of the room. The footballer had stood up, towering over the Smedleys.

"I'm not fucking wearing roller skates," he shouted.

"Oh dear," Alexander whispered to his teammate. "Trouble in paradise, already?"

Zac chuckled. "I don't blame him. Cooking on casters is not a good move. Almost as dangerous as cooking in the nude. I once had a very close call a fizzing fillet steak."

Alexander shuddered. "That's why I get a lovely young man on a moped to deliver my dinner. He doesn't care if I'm naked or not."

"Now that I would like to see."

The man that Amber Jade had spoken to approached them before Alexander could form a suitable response. "All right, lads?" he said. "I'm Darren Sprix, your camera man."

Of course, with reality television they couldn't just go off and do the actual task for a week. Everything would have to be captured on YouTube for future generations.

"What is our first assignment?" Zac asked.

"I'm not allowed to say yet," Darren replied with a smirk. "At least we're out and about. I didn't fancy spending a week in kitchens. Poor bastards."

Derek and Wayne stood glaring at each other with Dora trying to get in between them.

"Had a think about your blog name yet?" Darren continued.

Alexander stared across at Zac. Their eyes met and a frisson of electricity sent tingles up the back of Alexander's head. Zac's single status was public knowledge. His last relationship with a sheep farmer had ended over a year ago. It had been splashed all over the scandal rags. "How about *In At The Deep End?*" he said, not breaking Zac's gaze.

"I like it," Zac replied with a grin that would melt a dozen housewives' hearts. He pushed his glasses up on his nose and sat forward. "How far will you push yourself?"

Alexander didn't like the sound of this. When they had said new experiences, he had thought they meant the latest restaurant or perhaps a gig in a rough part of town. Zac stared at him with a glint in his eye.

He would not stand down from a dare. "Oh, I go all the way," Alexander replied, biting his lip.

"Good stuff," Darren said. "You boys go home and get some sleep. I'll have your first assignment to you by the morning."

Alexander drained his bottle of beer. "Fine," he said. "I'm allergic to nuts and I don't do children. Please try to remember that."

Darren chuckled. "Noted."

"I'd better call my driver then," Alexander said. "Can I drop you anywhere?"

"I'm good," Zac said, standing. "I'm at the Corinthia. It's only across the bridge."

Alexander appraised him a new light. The Corinthia was one of the best in town. Then it dawned on him. "Did the show pay for that?"

Zac made a face. "No, they wanted to put me up in some dosshouse. Not a chance, mate."

"I should think not," Alexander added. "We can't have the darling of the glens laying his head just anywhere."

Darren also stood. "I've got a good feeling about this team," he said.

Zac's eyes met Alexander's. "So have I," he said. "So have I."

TRADEMARKS

The author acknowledges the trademarked status and trademark owners of the following mentioned in this work of fiction:

Formula One – Formula One Licensing BV
Alcoholics Anonymous – A.A.W.S Inc
Maserati – Maserati S.p.A.
Aston Martin Roadster – Aston Martin Lagonda Limited
London Eye – Merlin Attractions Operations Ltd
The Shawshank Redemption – Castle Rock Entertainment
Grindr – Grindr LLC
James Bond – Danjaq LLC
Ferrari – Ferrari S.p.A.
Mary Poppins – Disney Enterprises Inc
Maleficent – Disney Enterprises Inc
Star Wars – Disney Enterprises Inc
The Beatles – Apple Corps Ltd
Claridges – Claridges Hotel Ltd